JUST HOPE

(A Cami Lark Mystery —Book Eight)

BLAKE PIERCE

Blake Pierce

Blake Pierce is the USA Today bestselling author of the RILEY PAGE mystery series, which includes seventeen books. Blake Pierce is also the author of the MACKENZIE WHITE mystery series, comprising fourteen books; of the AVERY BLACK mystery series, comprising six books; of the KERI LOCKE mystery series, comprising five books; of the MAKING OF RILEY PAIGE mystery series, comprising six books; of the KATE WISE mystery series, comprising seven books; of the CHLOE FINE psychological suspense mystery, comprising six books; of the JESSIE HUNT psychological suspense thriller series, comprising thirty-one books; of the AU PAIR psychological suspense thriller series, comprising three books; of the ZOE PRIME mystery series, comprising six books; of the ADELE SHARP mystery series, comprising sixteen books, of the EUROPEAN VOYAGE cozy mystery series, comprising six books; of the LAURA FROST FBI suspense thriller, comprising eleven books; of the ELLA DARK FBI suspense thriller, comprising twenty-one books (and counting); of the A YEAR IN EUROPE cozy mystery series, comprising nine books, of the AVA GOLD mystery series, comprising six books; of the RACHEL GIFT mystery series, comprising thirteen books (and counting); of the VALERIE LAW mystery series, comprising nine books (and counting); of the PAIGE KING mystery series, comprising eight books (and counting); of the MAY MOORE mystery series, comprising eleven books; of the CORA SHIELDS mystery series, comprising eight books (and counting); of the NICKY LYONS mystery series, comprising eight books (and counting), of the CAMI LARK mystery series, comprising nine books (and counting), of the AMBER YOUNG mystery series, comprising seven books (and counting), of the DAISY FORTUNE mystery series, comprising five books (and counting), of the FIONA RED mystery series, comprising nine books (and counting), of the FAITH BOLD mystery series, comprising eight books (and counting), of the JULIETTE HART mystery series, comprising five books (and counting), of the MORGAN CROSS mystery series, comprising seven books (and counting), and of the new FINN WRIGHT mystery series, comprising five books (and counting).

An avid reader and lifelong fan of the mystery and thriller genres, Blake loves to hear from you, so please feel free to visit www.blakepierceauthor.com to learn more and stay in touch.

ISBN: 978-1-0943-8272-2

LET HER BE (Book #2)
LET HER HOPE (Book #3)
LET HER WISH (Book #4)
LET HER LIVE (Book #5)
LET HER RUN (Book #6)
LET HER HIDE (Book #7)
LET HER BELIEVE (Book #8)
LET HER FORGET (Book #9)

DAISY FORTUNE MYSTERY SERIES
NEED YOU (Book #1)
CLAIM YOU (Book #2)
CRAVE YOU (Book #3)
CHOOSE YOU (Book #4)
CHASE YOU (Book #5)

AMBER YOUNG MYSTERY SERIES
ABSENT PITY (Book #1)
ABSENT REMORSE (Book #2)
ABSENT FEELING (Book #3)
ABSENT MERCY (Book #4)
ABSENT REASON (Book #5)
ABSENT SANITY (Book #6)
ABSENT LIFE (Book #7)

CAMI LARK MYSTERY SERIES
JUST ME (Book #1)
JUST OUTSIDE (Book #2)
JUST RIGHT (Book #3)
JUST FORGET (Book #4)
JUST ONCE (Book #5)
JUST HIDE (Book #6)
JUST NOW (Book #7)
JUST HOPE (Book #8)
JUST LEAVE (Book #9)

NICKY LYONS MYSTERY SERIES
ALL MINE (Book #1)
ALL HIS (Book #2)
ALL HE SEES (Book #3)

ALL ALONE (Book #4)
ALL FOR ONE (Book #5)
ALL HE TAKES (Book #6)
ALL FOR ME (Book #7)
ALL IN (Book #8)

CORA SHIELDS MYSTERY SERIES
UNDONE (Book #1)
UNWANTED (Book #2)
UNHINGED (Book #3)
UNSAID (Book #4)
UNGLUED (Book #5)
UNSTABLE (Book #6)
UNKNOWN (Book #7)
UNAWARE (Book #8)

MAY MOORE SUSPENSE THRILLER
NEVER RUN (Book #1)
NEVER TELL (Book #2)
NEVER LIVE (Book #3)
NEVER HIDE (Book #4)
NEVER FORGIVE (Book #5)
NEVER AGAIN (Book #6)
NEVER LOOK BACK (Book #7)
NEVER FORGET (Book #8)
NEVER LET GO (Book #9)
NEVER PRETEND (Book #10)
NEVER HESITATE (Book #11)

PAIGE KING MYSTERY SERIES
THE GIRL HE PINED (Book #1)
THE GIRL HE CHOSE (Book #2)
THE GIRL HE TOOK (Book #3)
THE GIRL HE WISHED (Book #4)
THE GIRL HE CROWNED (Book #5)
THE GIRL HE WATCHED (Book #6)
THE GIRL HE WANTED (Book #7)
THE GIRL HE CLAIMED (Book #8)

VALERIE LAW MYSTERY SERIES

NO MERCY (Book #1)
NO PITY (Book #2)
NO FEAR (Book #3)
NO SLEEP (Book #4)
NO QUARTER (Book #5)
NO CHANCE (Book #6)
NO REFUGE (Book #7)
NO GRACE (Book #8)
NO ESCAPE (Book #9)

RACHEL GIFT MYSTERY SERIES
HER LAST WISH (Book #1)
HER LAST CHANCE (Book #2)
HER LAST HOPE (Book #3)
HER LAST FEAR (Book #4)
HER LAST CHOICE (Book #5)
HER LAST BREATH (Book #6)
HER LAST MISTAKE (Book #7)
HER LAST DESIRE (Book #8)
HER LAST REGRET (Book #9)
HER LAST HOUR (Book #10)
HER LAST SHOT (Book #11)
HER LAST PRAYER (Book #12)
HER LAST LIE (Book #13)

AVA GOLD MYSTERY SERIES
CITY OF PREY (Book #1)
CITY OF FEAR (Book #2)
CITY OF BONES (Book #3)
CITY OF GHOSTS (Book #4)
CITY OF DEATH (Book #5)
CITY OF VICE (Book #6)

A YEAR IN EUROPE
A MURDER IN PARIS (Book #1)
DEATH IN FLORENCE (Book #2)
VENGEANCE IN VIENNA (Book #3)
A FATALITY IN SPAIN (Book #4)

ELLA DARK FBI SUSPENSE THRILLER

GIRL, ALONE (Book #1)
GIRL, TAKEN (Book #2)
GIRL, HUNTED (Book #3)
GIRL, SILENCED (Book #4)
GIRL, VANISHED (Book 5)
GIRL ERASED (Book #6)
GIRL, FORSAKEN (Book #7)
GIRL, TRAPPED (Book #8)
GIRL, EXPENDABLE (Book #9)
GIRL, ESCAPED (Book #10)
GIRL, HIS (Book #11)
GIRL, LURED (Book #12)
GIRL, MISSING (Book #13)
GIRL, UNKNOWN (Book #14)
GIRL, DECEIVED (Book #15)
GIRL, FORLORN (Book #16)
GIRL, REMADE (Book #17)
GIRL, BETRAYED (Book #18)
GIRL, BOUND (Book #19)
GIRL, REFORMED (Book #20)
GIRL, REBORN (Book #21)

LAURA FROST FBI SUSPENSE THRILLER
ALREADY GONE (Book #1)
ALREADY SEEN (Book #2)
ALREADY TRAPPED (Book #3)
ALREADY MISSING (Book #4)
ALREADY DEAD (Book #5)
ALREADY TAKEN (Book #6)
ALREADY CHOSEN (Book #7)
ALREADY LOST (Book #8)
ALREADY HIS (Book #9)
ALREADY LURED (Book #10)
ALREADY COLD (Book #11)

EUROPEAN VOYAGE COZY MYSTERY SERIES
MURDER (AND BAKLAVA) (Book #1)
DEATH (AND APPLE STRUDEL) (Book #2)
CRIME (AND LAGER) (Book #3)
MISFORTUNE (AND GOUDA) (Book #4)

CALAMITY (AND A DANISH) (Book #5)
MAYHEM (AND HERRING) (Book #6)

ADELE SHARP MYSTERY SERIES
LEFT TO DIE (Book #1)
LEFT TO RUN (Book #2)
LEFT TO HIDE (Book #3)
LEFT TO KILL (Book #4)
LEFT TO MURDER (Book #5)
LEFT TO ENVY (Book #6)
LEFT TO LAPSE (Book #7)
LEFT TO VANISH (Book #8)
LEFT TO HUNT (Book #9)
LEFT TO FEAR (Book #10)
LEFT TO PREY (Book #11)
LEFT TO LURE (Book #12)
LEFT TO CRAVE (Book #13)
LEFT TO LOATHE (Book #14)
LEFT TO HARM (Book #15)
LEFT TO RUIN (Book #16)

THE AU PAIR SERIES
ALMOST GONE (Book#1)
ALMOST LOST (Book #2)
ALMOST DEAD (Book #3)

ZOE PRIME MYSTERY SERIES
FACE OF DEATH (Book#1)
FACE OF MURDER (Book #2)
FACE OF FEAR (Book #3)
FACE OF MADNESS (Book #4)
FACE OF FURY (Book #5)
FACE OF DARKNESS (Book #6)

A JESSIE HUNT PSYCHOLOGICAL SUSPENSE SERIES
THE PERFECT WIFE (Book #1)
THE PERFECT BLOCK (Book #2)
THE PERFECT HOUSE (Book #3)
THE PERFECT SMILE (Book #4)
THE PERFECT LIE (Book #5)

THE PERFECT LOOK (Book #6)
THE PERFECT AFFAIR (Book #7)
THE PERFECT ALIBI (Book #8)
THE PERFECT NEIGHBOR (Book #9)
THE PERFECT DISGUISE (Book #10)
THE PERFECT SECRET (Book #11)
THE PERFECT FAÇADE (Book #12)
THE PERFECT IMPRESSION (Book #13)
THE PERFECT DECEIT (Book #14)
THE PERFECT MISTRESS (Book #15)
THE PERFECT IMAGE (Book #16)
THE PERFECT VEIL (Book #17)
THE PERFECT INDISCRETION (Book #18)
THE PERFECT RUMOR (Book #19)
THE PERFECT COUPLE (Book #20)
THE PERFECT MURDER (Book #21)
THE PERFECT HUSBAND (Book #22)
THE PERFECT SCANDAL (Book #23)
THE PERFECT MASK (Book #24)
THE PERFECT RUSE (Book #25)
THE PERFECT VENEER (Book #26)
THE PERFECT PEOPLE (Book #27)
THE PERFECT WITNESS (Book #28)
THE PERFECT APPEARANCE (Book #29)
THE PERFECT TRAP (Book #30)
THE PERFECT EXPRESSION (Book #31)

CHLOE FINE PSYCHOLOGICAL SUSPENSE SERIES
NEXT DOOR (Book #1)
A NEIGHBOR'S LIE (Book #2)
CUL DE SAC (Book #3)
SILENT NEIGHBOR (Book #4)
HOMECOMING (Book #5)
TINTED WINDOWS (Book #6)

KATE WISE MYSTERY SERIES
IF SHE KNEW (Book #1)
IF SHE SAW (Book #2)
IF SHE RAN (Book #3)
IF SHE HID (Book #4)

IF SHE FLED (Book #5)
IF SHE FEARED (Book #6)
IF SHE HEARD (Book #7)

THE MAKING OF RILEY PAIGE SERIES
WATCHING (Book #1)
WAITING (Book #2)
LURING (Book #3)
TAKING (Book #4)
STALKING (Book #5)
KILLING (Book #6)

RILEY PAIGE MYSTERY SERIES
ONCE GONE (Book #1)
ONCE TAKEN (Book #2)
ONCE CRAVED (Book #3)
ONCE LURED (Book #4)
ONCE HUNTED (Book #5)
ONCE PINED (Book #6)
ONCE FORSAKEN (Book #7)
ONCE COLD (Book #8)
ONCE STALKED (Book #9)
ONCE LOST (Book #10)
ONCE BURIED (Book #11)
ONCE BOUND (Book #12)
ONCE TRAPPED (Book #13)
ONCE DORMANT (Book #14)
ONCE SHUNNED (Book #15)
ONCE MISSED (Book #16)
ONCE CHOSEN (Book #17)

MACKENZIE WHITE MYSTERY SERIES
BEFORE HE KILLS (Book #1)
BEFORE HE SEES (Book #2)
BEFORE HE COVETS (Book #3)
BEFORE HE TAKES (Book #4)
BEFORE HE NEEDS (Book #5)
BEFORE HE FEELS (Book #6)
BEFORE HE SINS (Book #7)
BEFORE HE HUNTS (Book #8)

PROLOGUE

Her phone beeped again. With anxiety flaring, Vicky Anderson looked down. She'd been getting weird texts all morning. Normally she wouldn't be so worried, but after a breakup with her boyfriend two weeks ago and after having issues with her job that had earned her a disciplinary, it felt like she had a target painted on her forehead.

As if life had painted a target there.

The disciplinarian hadn't even been her fault, it had been a coworker messing up, but she'd been in charge, and she had to take the blame for the fact that delivery of expensive furniture had gone to the wrong destination, wasting days of time and hundreds of dollars of transportation costs.

Her boss had been so mad at her. She'd eventually turned and rushed out of the office to escape his shouting. It was that or burst into tears in front of him. Not the most constructive way to solve the situation, she knew that, but it was what she'd done. She'd gone out, headed down to the mall, walked around for a while, and had a coffee to calm herself.

Now, she guessed, she had to go back in and face the music.

It was freezing cold, a chilly, late fall day in Boston, with rain sluicing sideways, driven by a strong wind. And she was on the other side of the bridge crossing the Charles River. She'd marched over it angrily when setting out on her walk. It was a long way to go back when she wasn't dressed for the weather. When she'd come the other way, it had at least been dry. Now, she was regretting her impulsive decision to have her shoulder-length brown hair chopped short after the breakup. Her neck was freezing.

Shivering, trying to turn up the collar of her jacket for more protection, she started on her way back.

And as she did, her phone beeped again.

Her gut clenched as she glanced down because it was the same weird message she'd seen half an hour ago in the cafe where she'd holed up.

"I know where you are, pretty girl. I can see you because my powers allow me to. I'm tracking you via a special connection, a darker force that I've channeled. I love that hairstyle! I enjoy short hair."

That's what the first one had said, anyway. But staring down in consternation at this one, Vicky saw it held more detail.

"I know where you are walking, short-haired sweetheart. You're going out onto the bridge. I'm with you; I'm at your shoulder. Think of me as your little friendly ghost. We'll be able to meet!"

Fear dropped in Vicky's stomach like a stone. How was this possible? This person - a man from the sound of it and that he'd referred to her hairstyle, he couldn't know, could he? Could he? Was he following her?

She glanced around, scanning the gray street in consternation. There were people walking to and fro, but all with their heads bowed, not looking up, trying to get where they were going without being hit by the force of the storm.

Was it just a coincidence that the text messages had started coming in after her breakup and work issues? Or was someone intentionally trying to scare her?

Best just to get to the office, she thought, because that was real trouble waiting right there. She'd need to explain why she'd left, why she'd walked out after that harsh reprimand she'd received.

As she headed out onto the bridge, her feet clanging on the steel walkway and cars swishing past, she got another text.

"You're on the bridge now, pretty one? Well done! That's where we're going to meet. You and I, we have a date there. With destiny, you could say."

She froze, her breath caught in her throat. Was this a sick joke? She tried to rationalize it; maybe it was just someone who knew her ex and was pulling a cruel prank. But her gut told her something else. This was real, and it was dangerous.

It would be better to turn back. Or would it? Now, she didn't know what to do, and her phone was beeping again, the sound now making her blood pressure spike.

"Thinking of turning back? I see you're standing still now. I guess you're scared. Don't be. It's just a date. You've been on dates before, right?"

Vicky's mind was racing. Who could be doing this? Was it her ex? One of her coworkers? She didn't have any enemies that she knew of, but maybe she was wrong. Maybe she did.

2

A sound behind her made her jump. Was that someone sneaking up on her? She whirled around, but no one was there. Just the wind rattling through the steel supports of the bridge.

Who was this person? And how did they know so much about her? It was as if they were watching her every move.

She had to get back to work, and there was nobody on the bridge. Nobody at all. The pedestrian lane was clear. If she walked fast, she could be all the way to the other side in five minutes.

Vicky took a deep breath, not liking the idea, not liking any of the choices that she had in this increasingly weird situation. But she couldn't stay put because she was freezing to death. And she couldn't call a cab. Right now, she didn't want to be around any strangers, and besides, she was totally broke. Payday was in two days - if she got her salary check after this debacle.

"You need to get back to the office," she insisted to herself firmly.

Then, walking as fast as possible, she set out along the bridge.

One minute went by. Then another. She heard the tread of her footsteps, the puffs of her breath, the rustling of her jacket.

And then, her phone beeped again, sending a sickening jolt of anxiety through her.

"On the bridge? Good decision! You're too far to go back now! I am coming for you."

A gust of wind nearly shook her off her feet. Coming for her? What did he mean?

Shaking her head, she carried on walking, but her heart was in overdrive now, and she was feeling seriously scared. And then, another one.

"I'm going to sweep you off your feet. Literally. Want to know what that means?"

No, she didn't want to know that. She had no desire to know what that message meant; that sounded far more like a threat than a taunt.

Head down, she plowed on, but when the next message came, she couldn't stop herself from looking.

"I hope you enjoy broken bones. You're going to be suffering a few of them just now. Call it a psychic prediction."

What? What was this? Broken bones?

She stared around her wildly. Was he in a car? He must be in a car, and that meant he was going to be coming for her, and he would plow into her, and she would be crushed against the steel barricade or else knocked off the bridge and fall to her death.

Sickening fear pervaded her, and she made her decision. She was going to climb over the rail. She couldn't risk some madman crashing into her. The thought was filling her with horror. It would be better to jump down into the water. Yes, it was far below. But she could swim, she'd be okay, and at least she'd be away from him.

The water was a better bet than broken bones, than this reality of the threat that was filling her mind, driving all logic out of her thoughts. It was terrifying, terrifying in a way she couldn't even imagine. She'd always had nightmares about a bad person chasing her, and now they were coming true.

For a moment, she hesitated, looking at the gray water so far, far below, feeling her stomach twist. This was a bad idea, too. Maybe an even worse idea. She should call for help; that's what she should do.

But then, another beep from her phone made her jump, her hand moving instinctively to her purse, and at the same time a gust of wind battered her. Her foot slipped off the narrow steel rim and she gasped, dangling out over the water, flailing for purchase but realizing it was too late - she couldn't hold on.

And, as her grip slipped and she tumbled down through the cold, surging air, she realized how high she was.

So much higher than she'd thought. So much further to fall.

Then the gray water came rushing up, as solid as concrete, and she knew nothing more.

CHAPTER ONE

In a week - one short week - everything had changed.

Everything.

Cami Lark was sitting cross-legged on the two-seater couch in the tiny living room. On the side where it wasn't shaven, her black-dyed hair was hooked behind her ear to keep it out of the way as she worked on her laptop. She was still wearing her gray dressing gown and her blue pajamas, and her black fluffy socks.

On the third floor of the building, the only view from the living room window was the opposite building, although she felt connected to the street below by the sounds that traveled upward and the aromas that wafted in from the Chinese takeout shop on the corner.

Now, at eight in the morning, she'd taken a half-finished box of chicken chow mein out of the refrigerator and was eating occasional bites of the cold but fragrant food while she worked.

She felt as if she was on a life-or-death mission here.

The image still flared in her mind, making her pulse race and her anxiety surge when she thought about it.

She'd been on her way to Liam Treverton's house. She'd thought that she would get more answers from the ex-FBI agent on her sister Jenna's disappearance. Cami had discovered recently that he'd been the agent who had first been assigned the case after Jenna had vanished from home six years ago, and it had been escalated to the FBI.

Her father, the bullying cop, had always downplayed it, labeling Jenna a runaway. But Cami had always known, passionately, that there was more to it and that Jenna must have been taken.

At the time, she'd thought the FBI hadn't taken it seriously. Then when she'd relooked at it, she'd been furious, thinking that Liam hadn't taken it seriously and had deliberately botched it.

Now, having delved into the matter more closely, she was concluding something different. Liam had been investigating it thoroughly but had been removed from the case. Abruptly and deliberately. And he'd quit the FBI not long afterward.

Reckoning that a face-to-face meeting was the best way to question this clearly frightened man, she'd thought that she'd organized it discreetly, using her hacking abilities to log into his home's smart communication hub and leave a message on the screen.

Then at the last minute, the venue had changed. A message had been sent back to her that had told her to come to his house instead of to the public meeting spot they'd arranged.

Cami had smelled a rat, and she'd logged into his home camera system just to check. She didn't want to walk into a trap, and that was exactly what she would have done.

The camera in the bedroom had shown her that Liam had been lying on his bed, and she still couldn't get that gruesome picture out of her mind, nor the mental shockwaves that accompanied it.

He'd been dead. His head had been bloody. He'd been violently, recently attacked, and now she had no idea who had left that message about the changed venue. Was it him or his killer? She suspected it had been the killer. If so, did the killer know who she was?

There was so much she didn't know, but she was doing her best to find it out, even though it now felt like treading deeper into danger every step of the way.

"How's it going?"

The voice came from behind her, and from the tiny kitchenette, Cami now smelled coffee.

She turned, distracted from her research. There was Kieran, picking his way over the scatter cushion that had ended up on the floor with two steaming cups in his hand.

"Oh, thanks," she said gratefully. Kieran made brilliant coffee.

Tall, dark, handsome, and surprisingly similar to his brother Ethan in so many ways, Cami had never, ever thought a month ago that she'd be sharing an apartment with him.

She'd met Ethan at the FBI after being caught out hacking their website and being forced to enter into an 'agreement' to help them with cases for a year. Not that there had been much chance to disagree when the alternative was a prison sentence.

At first, she'd hated her boss, and investigation partner, Connor. She'd seen him as a domineering father figure, similar to her own dad, and she'd hated every minute of working with him. But when she'd met Ethan, who was on Connor's team, his love for his job, his respect for his team, and his commitment to doing good, had changed her mind about a lot of things.

She'd fallen for Ethan hard.

And then, while they were following Jenna's trail, while they were out at a bar, getting a voice recording to open the computer which she'd stolen from Liam - they'd been followed and Ethan had been shot.

Now, Liam had been killed, too, and Cami was under no illusions that she might be targeted next if whoever was doing this knew who she was. Whatever was going on, they were killing everyone involved. Everyone who knew.

She wished she knew what it was that was being covered up. She'd been shocked to hear from Kieran that Ethan had been investigating something 'at work' before he was shot. He'd been trying to expose something, and that was why they'd taken him out.

But was it connected with Jenna? That was what she now suspected, but she didn't know for sure. Was this all intertwined, and if so, how?

She'd felt safe at MIT, where she'd been completing her degree in computer science, but she'd written her last exam a week ago and had needed to move out. And Kieran had very kindly offered for her to share his apartment. He'd started renting it a month ago. With his mechanical engineering degree completed, he'd gotten work with a project team that was doing upgrades on the ventilation and air conditioning systems in clinics and hospitals throughout the city.

Cami could afford to pay her share of the rent. The FBI had paid her for the cases she'd done so far, quite generously, and she'd also been doing some online tuition, helping a few high school kids with their computer studies while she waited for her exam results and got ready to make a firm decision about the next step in her life.

The problem was that she couldn't exactly apply for a full-time job when she might be called away to help with an FBI case at any given time. That wouldn't sit well with a new employer.

She'd even considered the possibility - just toyed with the idea - of joining the FBI full-time. Could she do that?

She hadn't thought about it too hard, though, because Cami was suspecting that whatever was going on with Ethan involved someone at the FBI. Joining now might get her noticed. It might make her an easier target. At least now, in this small apartment just a couple of miles from MIT, in a crowded and fun part of town where students and young professionals lived, she felt like she could hole up and stay safe.

"Cami, are you sure you're okay sleeping on the couch every night?" Kieran asked her, his hazel eyes bright and concerned as they stared into her green ones, his strong-boned face framed by dark hair.

"Oh, yes, I'm fine," she said hurriedly. "I'm absolutely fine on the couch."

"We could at least take turns? Like, one week on, one week off? I feel like you need to sleep in a bed sometimes."

Cami shook her head. "I'm really okay."

The truth was that she was trying to make sure she didn't fall for Kieran. Because they'd shared a lot together since he'd contacted her after Ethan's death, looking to tell her what he knew. They liked each other. He was twenty-three, just two years older than her. He was smart, and he was brave, and she'd come to admire him a lot in the couple of weeks she'd spent here. He was hardworking, funny, caring, and he was even teaching her to cook. He had about five different meals in his repertoire for the nights when they didn't get Chinese. That was five more than she had.

She didn't want him to know how much she liked him. What if it complicated things? What if he didn't have the same feelings for her? That was partly why she was wearing her pajamas and dressing gown now, even though there had been an opportunity to change into jeans and a nice top. She thought it was safer. She knew the pajamas were especially unattractive, and the dressing gown made her look like a big gray fluffy bear, effectively covering up her slim, compact figure. As for the socks, the less said about them, the better.

"What are you finding?" he asked. Now he sounded anxious, too. He was also invested in this. He'd told her that Ethan had had an attempt on his life before. He'd been shot at a couple of months back when walking with Kieran.

They might both be targets. Who knew what would happen?

"I'm searching for hidden email folders," she told him. "I think Liam has a lot of layers of security on this machine. I got into some of them, but now I'm seeing traces that there might be more, even better hidden. So I'm tunneling down with a program I use that's very good at finding hidden files, but you have to point it in the right direction. And it takes time."

"I've been watching the news," Kieran said. "There hasn't been much about - about what happened to Liam. From what I saw, they are treating it as a botched robbery. They're thinking someone broke in to steal stuff. A few things were missing, apparently. A few valuables."

Cami nodded. That didn't surprise her. Whoever was behind this was smart. But she was sure it wasn't a robbery.

"I don't think that's correct," she said.

"Me, either," he nodded.

And then, the computer pinged, and her focus sharpened.

"Look here," she said, pointing. "It's in. It's found something that was hidden, Kieran!"

CHAPTER TWO

"This surely must tell us something!" Cami couldn't hold back the words as she stared down at the folder. It was buried in a sub-folder, in a section of the machine's archives that she would never have thought would have had anything hidden.

Liam had squirreled it carefully away out of sight in the manner of someone who needed to keep it hidden at all costs.

A careful man.

Or maybe not. Maybe a frightened man.

She drew in a sharp breath as she saw what was inside.

"Kieran, look. This is a series of emails he's sent to himself. Like a backup of his work."

Kieran leaned in closer to the screen, scanning the contents of the folder. "This is definitely something. But what is it? It doesn't look like there's anything there."

His hair tickled Cami's cheek. She quickly moved aside, away from that light, fluttering touch.

The emails were dated from a month after Jenna's disappearance. And they continued up until two years ago. That would have been soon after Liam left the FBI.

"He was sending himself backup emails after Jenna's case and even after he left the FBI," she explained.

"You said he left under a cloud?"

"Yes. There was something very irregular about the entire process. I think he was basically forced out," Cami explained. "The question is, why?"

"He didn't have a disciplinary hearing, anything wrong?"

She shook her head. "There are notes that I found earlier when looking online, that said something about him being 'disgraced.' But I could never work out why." She turned and stared at Kieran, feeling hope surge inside her that they might finally be getting closer to solving this deadly and heartbreaking puzzle.

"Maybe he wasn't disgraced, then? That's the simplest answer. Maybe someone just wanted to make it seem that way."

"Maybe he didn't have a choice," Cami said thoughtfully. "Because if he had been unfairly kicked out, why wouldn't he fight it? That's what anyone would do, right? If you're unfairly dismissed from a big organization after doing your job to the best of your ability, then why wouldn't you take action back at them?"

Looking at him, she could see that he was reaching exactly the same conclusion she was.

"You wouldn't fight it if you'd been threatened. If you'd been told to back off, or else," Kieran said. "What do these emails say?"

"The content is still being populated," Cami explained. "It's very fragmented. Liam did a really great job of making sure that folder was hidden, and he might even have done a basic delete on it since then. I don't know how much of the actual content we'll get. Some might be missing."

She waited, watching, as the list built, infinitesimally slowly.

For a few moments, the only noise was the sound of their quiet breathing.

"Have you asked anyone in the FBI about this?" Kieran said.

Cami shook her head. "I promised my boss, Connor, that I would. He told me I must ask my parole officer, Jacinta."

"Parole officer?" Kieran sounded startled.

"I was also surprised," she admitted. "Apparently, you get issued one after being caught hacking the FBI's homepage. But anyway, Connor told me that she'd be the one who would be able to advise me in a confidential way. In a way that wouldn't be dangerous to me because if there's something going on and the wrong person hears about it..."

She shook her head, that bloody sight coming back into her mind, the vision etched in her memory.

Liam's face, those wide eyes, the blood spreading and staining the white covers.

She'd hated Liam at first when she'd found out who he was and had believed that he'd botched the case. Now she was realizing the truth was very different and far darker. Liam had been one of the good guys. At any rate, he hadn't been one of the bad guys, and she wished she'd known that earlier.

"So, have you asked Jacinta?"

Cami shook her head. "Something like this, I couldn't do it on the phone. I want to be with her face-to-face somewhere. Just in case. It seems safer."

He nodded. "Agreed."

"I was too - too traumatized after seeing what I saw for a couple of days. Then, I was busy writing my final exam. Then I was moving. Great timing, hey. At least I got somewhere to stay, thanks to you."

A smile briefly warmed the serious expression on his face.

"So I called her a few days ago, and she's on leave. She's getting back tomorrow, and as soon as she is back, we're going to meet."

Cami could see clearly in her mind the dark-haired, dark-eyed woman who'd been such a source of support and advice to her during her often troubled time with the FBI. Jacinta had been a tower of strength. She was sharp, savvy, and Cami respected her hugely. She hoped that over the months, Jacenta had come to regard her differently because she knew at the beginning, she'd felt Cami to be a little upstart and a troublemaker, who was just going to cause more problems than she solved.

She'd tried her best to earn some respect and some friendship - probably more than she deserved after her rocky start.

"Here is one. Look, we have the first one," she said.

She leaned forward, clicking on it, reading it.

"I've been told to drop the case," she read.

Shivers chilled their way down her spine. She was reading what Liam had written a few years ago while doing his best to find out what had happened to her older sister and why she'd disappeared. Her dad, domineering and disapproving, had always thought Jenna to be a runaway. It was Cami who believed, passionately and with all her heart, that even if Jenna had run away, she'd have said goodbye first.

"Who's he writing that to?"

"It looks like it is an official email to his superior. A guy called Bill. That's all I can make out from this." Cami kept reading. "I've been told to drop the case, and I'd like to question why. I've been making progress and have traced that Jenna Lark was seen the day before her disappearance, speaking to a man that a witness can describe. Tall, dark-haired, with a short haircut, and with a gun in a holster."

Cami broke off, her eyes now widening further, as she swung around to Kieran.

"Does that sound to you like it might have been FBI?"

"It sounds like something of the sort," Kieran agreed.

"So then, he wrote that he wants to pursue this lead and that it's very important, and that an individual like this might be traceable. I can see that he also thought there was something strange going on. You can just tell it from his language. I feel like he's thinking his back's already against the wall because there's something not right happening."

Cami couldn't wait to read more. What had the boss said? Who was this Bill anyway, and how could she find out?

"It's going slow again. We need to give it a few hours. There's a gap here," she said, disappointed. "But as it searches, it might fill in that gap. I'm hoping so. We need to find this out."

She could see that Kieran felt the same, his face was intent, and his mind was also working furiously as he tried to figure out what this might mean and what the implications were.

Like a threatening shadow in the distance, Cami thought she could make out some of the missing pieces, and she wasn't liking them. They were scary. And they felt like they were part of something way bigger than her. People had killed to keep these secrets, and she was sure they would kill again.

The sound of her phone ringing almost made her hit the roof; she jumped so hard. Kieran spilled his coffee at the sound, sending a splash of it onto the coffee table. Quickly, he scrambled up and went to fetch a cloth.

It was Connor on the line, and Cami immediately swiped up the call.

"Cami," her boss - part-time anyway - said. "How are you doing? Your exams are over now?"

"Yes, they are," she said. "They went okay. I'm doing okay. I'm in a shared apartment now."

She could tell from the tone of his voice that this wasn't just a social call, and his next words confirmed it.

"We've got a case. It's very puzzling, and we need your tech expertise to help solve it. How quickly can you get in here?"

Cami checked the time.

"I'll call a cab," she said. "I can be there by half past eight."

"Hurry."

The one quick, decisive word told Cami that this case was serious. And that they needed her, fast.

CHAPTER THREE

"I have to go," Cami told Kieran. "It's Connor, my contact at the FBI. There's a new case on the go."

She saw mixed emotions flicker over his face. That was okay. She felt them, too. She was also deeply uneasy about the FBI at this point. However, her unease did not extend to Connor.

"I trust Connor," she told him. "He's a good guy. He's the best. No way is he caught up in this."

Kieran frowned. "You sure, Cami?"

Connor's tough face, his hard eyes, his short, brown hair graying at the temples, flitted into Cami's mind. He was a bulldog of a man when it came to hunting out the truth, and he was as fair and upfront as anyone she'd known.

And Ethan had trusted him completely.

"He's good," she said. "He's a good man. The best."

It was just everyone else in the FBI that had a question mark over them at this point.

"Please, just be careful," Kieran emphasized.

"I will," she promised.

"This computer. Must I do anything to it?"

She shook her head. "Just leave it plugged in so that the battery doesn't run down. When the program finishes up, it will automatically turn off. That's okay because I can turn it back on."

"This case. I guess it might take a while?"

"Yes. I might be back tonight if it's local, or tomorrow, or maybe even later than that. I don't know anything about it."

She was rummaging through her clothes - which occupied the first two shelves of Kieran's bookcase - looking for a spare shirt, some underwear, some extra socks, and her toiletry bag. She saw Kieran averting his eyes in a gentlemanly way to give her some privacy as she packed these personal items into her laptop bag, together with the spare laptop that she'd bought, especially for her FBI cases. It was powerful, but it was smaller and more portable than the big, state-of-the-art machine she used for her coding. That coding machine was precious.

And Cami knew that when she went out on a case, they often ended up in risky situations, so she'd invested in a second one.

Then, she called up a cab, which she saw would take just three minutes to arrive.

And then she was all done. It only remained to grab her FBI jacket off the coat hook in the hallway.

"Bye for now," she said to Kieran, who'd walked through with her.

"Bye," he said.

She didn't want to, she was so conflicted, but she couldn't help it. She stepped forward and hugged him and felt him hug her in turn, instantly. His arms wrapped around her, very tight and very hard.

They hugged a few moments longer than Cami felt was strictly necessary. But she couldn't make herself stop.

Finally, she lowered her arms, and only then, so did he.

"Be careful," he said.

"I will try my best to be. And you must, too," she said, feeling a sudden flare of worry about him being on his own here. He'd been out there when Ethan was targeted. Who knew how far these people would go?

She wanted to say something more to him but didn't know what would be the right thing, and in any case, the cab was coming.

Cami grabbed her FBI jacket off the coat hook and put it on. She took the navy blue baseball cap off another hook and pulled that down tightly over her head, concealing her edgy hairstyle. It brought to mind the way that Connor had looked disapprovingly at her hair on the first case she'd helped with. Now, she didn't think he even noticed it, but she wore the cap all the same because she'd learned that sometimes it helped not to look too recognizable.

With just thirty seconds until her cab pulled up, she turned and hustled down the corridor. She raced down the stairs and rushed out of the lobby at exactly the moment it arrived.

As soon as she was inside, she checked her phone again.

No more texts from Connor. She'd have to wait until she reached the FBI offices to know more.

Cami sat back and tried to calm her thoughts as the cab pulled onto the main street. She needed to focus on the case and on what she might need to do to solve a serious crime.

She didn't need to focus on how it had felt with Kieran's arms around her. Or on the fact that now, going into the FBI offices felt as if she was entering enemy territory.

*

Ten minutes later, there she was. Climbing out of the cab at the Boston FBI offices in Beech Street, Chelsea, was familiar to her now. She even recognized the guard at the security checkpoint.

"Hello, Ms. Lark," he greeted her, with a familiarity in his voice that made her feel they were on first-name terms despite the polite use of her last name.

"Hello, Tomms," she greeted him likewise, wondering what his first name even was. Then she started wondering if he'd checked in one of the people who'd killed Liam. Or Ethan. That made her feel uneasy all over again.

She gave him a last, quick nod of thanks and hurried down the corridor to Connor's offices.

The door was ajar, but she tapped on it anyway as a courtesy, already seeing him inside.

"Cami," he said, raising his head from a case file. She saw how his face warmed when he saw her.

Two months ago, Cami would have rolled her eyes at the sight of all that paperwork, believing Connor to be a dinosaur. Now, she understood better that this was how he worked and felt comfortable. He wasn't a tech guru, but he sure could delve down into human nature, crime scenarios, and people's motives better than any artificial intelligence could do.

"Connor," she said, walking in and sitting down opposite.

"Are you okay? You safe?" His gaze sharpened. "You spoken to Jacenta yet?"

She shook her head. "There was - there was a small complication. Then I had exams. And then she's been away. We're meeting tomorrow."

She wished she could tell Connor about the 'small complication' of the murder. But chances were it hadn't even crossed the radar of anyone at the FBI who was innocent of the motives behind it. After all, it had been set up as a botched robbery, and individual crimes like this were not handled by the FBI. If Liam had still been an agent, that would have been different, but Liam was no longer an agent.

So Cami couldn't say a thing about it.

"It's well overdue," Connor grumbled, and she could see from his expression that his grumpiness was actually due to being worried about

16

her. That wasn't something she'd have picked up back when she joined. It was a personal skill she'd learned along the way. She guessed that meant she was growing. Developing other attributes than being lightning-fast at coding and hacking.

"So anyway," he said. "This case."

"Go on?" Cami wanted to know what this was about. What would she and Connor be getting themselves into this time?

"It's two cases, actually. They aren't officially linked, but the police called us in because they are in the same area, and both seem rather - inexplicable, I guess."

"How's that?"

"The first one was a woman who strayed onto a construction site. She ended up walking out on the scaffolding over a deep excavation pit and then fell. She landed on her head and, unfortunately, died instantly."

"And the second one?" Cami asked.

"The second was a woman who climbed over the bridge railing and fell into the Charles River. She drowned. She might have landed badly and passed out. It was a long way up," Connor said in a tone that chilled her. "That was yesterday. The other one was the day before. So they're both recent."

Cami paused. Waited. Was any more information forthcoming? But it seemed not.

"They couldn't both be suicides?" she asked. "It sounds like suicide. These falls. They couldn't have been intentional jumps?"

Connor nodded. "It's possible. Never say never. But neither victim had any history of suicide or depression, although the second one seems to have been going through a few challenges from what this case file tells us. Neither one left a note. The entire situation is just ringing alarm bells, and the police want to check it out."

"I guess the camera footage might show something?" she asked.

Connor nodded. "The footage from the bridge is being obtained. It's likely to be low quality, so anything you can do to enhance it will help. But the footage from the construction site is not available yet. They're stalling. There are cameras there, and they seem to be working, so I'm guessing the reason is that they have been doing a few things irregularly and don't want the police getting any proof of that." He paused, looking at Cami meaningfully. "There might be other ways of getting to view that footage. Just to give us some background and a better picture of what played out."

Cami knew immediately what he meant. If the site management was unwilling to let them in, she'd need to hack her way into the systems while they were standing at the gate.

That would mean working fast.

"I'm ready," she said, hoping that the new program she'd written to crack the password would stand up to its first real test.

CHAPTER FOUR

As soon as Cami arrived at the construction site, with Connor following, she could see that this was an unwelcoming place. It wasn't just the Keep Out notice, hand painted in red on white at the gate; it was also the threatening glare of the guard standing beyond.

The site was close to the Charles River and to the center of town, not far from where the other victim had fallen to her death. It looked to be a massive excavation where she guessed more warehouses, with basement areas, were going to be built. For now, though, it was partly a huge hole, partly tall scaffolding, and partly half-built walls.

"FBI," Connor said, showing his badge.

The guard stepped forward, looking defensive and obstructive.

"Sir, we've had the police here already. We don't want any further liability problems on site."

"We need access to your cameras," Connor said.

"I'll call my manager," the guard said.

Without opening the gate, which was firmly closed and locked with a padlock on the inside, he turned and strode away toward the heart of the activity, where several workers were constructing a wall and two excavators were hard at work beyond.

"The gate was open yesterday and also last week," Connor muttered. "We guess that's how the victim got in. She just walked into the site after hours when they were packing up. But more than that, only the footage will say."

Sure enough, Cami could see the camera installed on a pole and pointed directly at the scaffolding. She had a suspicion that it was there to ensure the workers didn't shirk their jobs or steal any equipment. That was her gut feeling. It seemed to her like that kind of a place.

"I'm going to see what I can get," she said, discreetly edging behind Connor as she got out her phone. What could she find here? What were the cameras connected up to?

As she started to hunt for a wifi connection, she heard an angry voice shout out.

"Sir, we must ask you to vacate the site. It's private property! We've had the police here!"

"We need to see your footage," Connor said to the angry manager, who was striding up briskly. He was short and squat, wearing a very old, torn work overall and a very new, shiny hard hat.

"I came to ask you yesterday. I'm asking again today."

"The footage is private. It's for internal use only," the man insisted.

"We need to see how the incident occurred," Connor pressured him. But he placed his hands on his hips angrily.

"It occurred because we had a member of the public trespassing. That's it; it's as simple as that. The footage will prove that she just wandered onto the site. Do you think we brought her here? I'm not even sure what you are thinking!"

"Sir, wc'rc not saying that you brought hcr hcrc," Connor said calmly. "We just need to see what happened. If it was an accident, then that's that. But we need to rule out any foul play."

The man glared at Connor, his eyes narrowing in suspicion.

"We have had an accident-free site for years, and I don't want any liability claims. You're going to muddy the waters here if you get involved."

While Connor argued with the manager, Cami had logged into the cameras.

She'd gotten the wifi password very fast and was proud of the program she'd written to do this. She'd tweaked it and fine-tuned it, especially for use in these situations when the time was limited, and she needed to get access fast. And it had performed brilliantly. She used a combination of brute force techniques, together with a clever piece of software that fooled some wifi systems into granting immediate access when it was used. But it wasn't needed here. The password was quite basic, and her brute force attempt succeeded almost immediately. This manager seemed a lot better at protecting his premises through bullying tactics than he did through strong IT precautions.

Now, what could she find?

Narrowing her eyes, Cami quickly transferred to the backup tape from yesterday, running it backward to see what had happened, and copying it as she went, because she didn't know how much time she'd have within range of this weak wifi signal. There she was. She risked a glance down as Connor faced off yet again with the manager. She guessed that he was just buying her time here so that she could do what she needed to do.

She didn't even have time to do more than glance down at it as the footage sped by, with the copying software faithfully duplicating the

20

hours of taping. She was going to go back three days, just in case they needed some extra time, she decided.

"I'm going to have to ask you to leave. Now!" the manager said.

"That's not going to work for us," Connor stood firm. "Unless you can give me a specific time when we can come in here and take a look at this footage."

The manager shifted from foot to foot, and Cami had a sudden strong impression that he was going to go and delete the footage. She guessed they'd only just been in time. There was something here that he didn't want them to see, that was for sure. But was it related to the woman's death?

"You can come in tomorrow," he relented. "Tomorrow after work. We're knocking off early tomorrow. But I must warn you that the footage has been very unreliable. I'm not sure how much of it will even be available."

Yup, for sure she was right, Cami thought. He'd been intending to erase it. But for now, they had it. She'd successfully made the copy.

"I guess that'll work fine," she said from behind Connor so that he would know she was done.

"We'll do that," Connor agreed.

He turned away. They walked back to the car.

As soon as they were inside, Cami got her laptop open and took a look at what she'd discovered, playing the footage back from the two on-site security cameras.

As soon as it began, Connor snorted.

"No wonder they didn't want us seeing it," he said. "Look at this. There are no hard hats there on site; someone's smoking and it even looks as if those two guys there are having a beer. Very badly managed. I'm sure he was going to erase that footage." He paused, adding thoughtfully, "If they'd been wider awake, then this might not have happened. If they'd been running an efficient site, then the team might have seen this woman, Pippa Ross, before she got up on that scaffolding."

So, what had happened?

Cami fast-forwarded the footage, and she and Connor watched intently, playing through hours of machines zooming back and forth and men scrambling swiftly up the scaffolding, hammers working at the speed of light, and then shimmying back down.

"Look," Cami said. She'd seen the flash of something at the edge of the screen. She slowed the footage to normal speed, and they both watched intently.

There was the victim, Pippa Ross. She was hurrying toward the site with her back to the camera. Cami noticed how as she approached, she glanced behind her, her face fearful.

Was someone chasing her? That was her first thought. That was what the woman's body language was telling her.

Then, Cami watched, astounded, as she made for the scaffolding and started to hurry across it as if she wanted to get to the other side of that yawning gap in the ground. But she never made it. She slipped, tried to save herself, and as Cami gasped in horror, she watched the woman fall.

Only then did the two men who'd been sharing a smoke and a beer on site look up. Perhaps she'd screamed as she'd fallen, Cami thought.

It was terrible seeing that. She closed her eyes for a moment, feeling sick. Watching someone fall to their death? How she wished she'd been able to rewind actual time and save her.

"That's all there is?" Connor sounded puzzled.

Cami swallowed hard and then reran the footage. The first camera only showed the woman. Nobody else came into the frame afterward. And the second camera hadn't picked her up at all.

Connor shook his head.

"This is strange. It doesn't really tell us anything." He sounded even more puzzled than he had before looking at the footage. "Do you think she could have done it as a dare?"

But Cami was checking it more closely.

"I think I see something," she said. "But I'm not totally sure. What could confirm it is if we can see the other footage. Is that ready?"

Connor checked his phone. "It is. Let's go back to the FBI office and take a look."

Cami closed her laptop as Connor started the car.

She felt thoroughly intrigued by what she'd glimpsed, but it wasn't enough. Now to see if the other footage from the fall off the bridge confirmed that moment and her suspicions.

CHAPTER FIVE

Back at the FBI office, Cami felt less exposed when walking in with Connor than she had been alone. And, with the thought of examining that footage, her mind was fully focused on the job that lay ahead.

"So, this other footage is the unclear one," Connor said. "It arrived just after we left. I haven't had a look at it, but the city was very apologetic about it. It's an old, faulty camera and it hasn't been replaced because they were waiting for budget. But maybe you can make out something."

He glanced at her questioningly, and she knew he was wondering - what had she seen in the first lot of footage?

She wasn't ready to say because she didn't want to go off on a tangent or make a wrong early connection. That was thanks to Connor's training. Connor had been the person who'd taught her not to jump to conclusions until you had sufficient evidence. Let the evidence lead you.

It was a very calm-minded way of going about investigating, and Cami could see why the cases that Connor presented were rock solid by the time they ended up in court. And it was amazing how working with him seemed to instill the same ethos in her own approach. She'd even found it helpful in her coding.

Connor opened his computer - a clunky dinosaur compared to her small, speedy spare one - and swiveled it around so she could see it.

"Can you forward it to me?" Cami asked immediately. Working on the dinosaur would just be annoying, and besides, the programs she needed were all on her own, faster machine.

While Connor did that, she watched the first lot of unedited footage, and so did he, frowning in an increasingly worried way as the blurry, grainy fog scrolled by.

"They weren't exaggerating when they said it was unclear," he commented. "You think you can get anything from this?"

It was a poor-quality picture, streaked and seamed with lines, and it bounced around, clearly unstable as the camera was jiggled by the wind.

"I guess it's a test of the software," she said.

She could see a figure going out onto the bridge, but that was about all. There was no way of telling if it was a man or a woman, tall or short, and as it retreated away along the bridge, Cami could only just make out the moment when this victim, Vicky Anderson, had climbed over and fallen to her death.

Even so, it gave her a stomach-churning flash of panic to look at her falling. What had happened there?

How terrible was it to actually watch footage of two women plummeting to their death? She wiped her palms on her jeans and breathed deeply as she turned to her own computer, readying herself to see it in sharper focus if her program worked.

If Cami's suspicions were right, then she wouldn't need to watch all the way to the end, though. She wouldn't need to wait until that last awful moment. She could stop the footage earlier, and then she could tell Connor what she'd found.

As the footage played, she leaned closer to the screen, her eyes scanning every detail of the video. It was much sharper now. Her software had done an incredible job of improving it. She still couldn't make out the features clearly, but she could see the hair blowing in the wind, and also she could clearly see Vicky's arms. That was what she needed.

"It's like night and day," Connor remarked, sounding impressed.

Cami scrolled through, watching carefully from the moment the woman came into view. You could see her much more clearly now and make out the way that the wind tugged at her hair and her jacket. And you could see the way that her arm turned, angling up, as she confirmed Cami's suspicions.

"It's the same," she said, surprised. "The same in both videos."

"What's the same?" Connor asked.

"Look here."

Cami called the footage up from both the cameras and played them side by side.

She paused the footage at the point where she'd seen both women doing the same recognizable, instinctive action.

"Look here. They're both checking their phones," she said. "It's as if they were reading messages - or reading some incoming information - along the way. Here, you can see. Vicky did it twice. No, in fact, three times. And then, look. She reads the message and climbs over the

24

railing. As if she was getting some kind of threat, or some kind of command, or some - something."

She shook her head. It was weird beyond belief that these two women had both done this.

"So, we need to see what they were reading," Connor said.

"Yes," Cami agreed. "Are either of those phones available?"

Connor shook his head. "Not Pippa's. It was completely damaged when she fell. Crushed under her, and it landed on a jagged piece of rebar. They've got the pieces of it with her clothing and personal belongings, but that's all." He paused. "Now that we know where Vicky fell and that she had her phone with her, we can send a diver down to look for it. It'll have been underwater a long time, though."

"We still might get something from it," she said.

"We can also get the transcripts of the texts from the service provider. They do keep records, but that's a time-consuming exercise." Connor sighed. "Best case, we're looking at about three to four business days, and there's no way of hurrying it. So for now, the phone is the best bet."

"Both the phones," Cami insisted.

"Both the phones," Connor agreed.

He paused, staring at her, and Cami knew with a twist of her stomach what was coming. It wasn't something she could avoid.

"We'll need to go to the pathology lab," he said. "And while we do that, I'm going to get on the phone and organize for the police scuba divers to search the bottom of the river and see what they can find."

Cami nodded. She knew she had to do this as part of the job, even though the thought of seeing a body filled her with sheer panic. That was because of Jenna. Thinking of a dead body, the finality of death, looking at wounds and injuries and those staring eyes, made her feel sick with panic at the thought of what might have befallen Jenna, how she might have died alone and without her family and friends knowing anything about it.

As that situation became clearer to Cami, as she saw what had happened to Ethan and to Liam, the knowledge was now settling heavy in her heart that Jenna was dead.

She must be. She'd somehow gotten involved with some very, very evil people, and Cami knew that it might only be possible now to avenge her death rather than find her sister alive. That was the harsh truth of it.

"With both the phones, we've got double the chance," she said, forcing herself to be strong as she closed her laptop and stood up. Connor glanced at her, admiration in his face as well as surprise as he heard her firm tone.

"Let's go there now," she added. "That phone might not be as crushed as they think it is."

CHAPTER SIX

Of course, Cami began regretting her decision as soon as she was out of Connor's office. What had she been thinking? Was she insane? No way did she want to go to the pathologist's office and look at the bodies of two women who'd died in a terrible way. Women that she'd actually seen on camera falling to their death. She knew that memory, the moments of watching that footage, would stay in her mind and haunt her nightmares for a long time to come.

As she followed Connor to the car, flat-footed, Cami acknowledged that the main reason she was forcing herself to be so strong and to face up to this, was her current circumstances. Whatever was going on, she was going to need to be as tough and capable as she could be to handle it.

She climbed into the car, thinking of Ethan with love and regret.

But then, as Connor drove onto the main road, she began to remember how Kieran's arms had felt around her, how he'd hugged her tightly, how they'd laughed together and shared warm bottles of cider while they'd cooked two nights ago because both of them had thought the other had put the cider into the refrigerator. How Kieran had taught her to chop onions in a way that was supposed to mean you didn't cry, only she'd done it wrong, and they'd both ended up in fits of giggles, with tears streaming down their faces.

Kieran was a very special guy. He was - she had to admit - a pretty amazing and strong human. And if he was going to stay alive and out of danger, then she needed to be strong too.

"You're doing well, Cami," Connor said as he headed along the familiar route to the pathologists' offices. "You're doing really well. I'm impressed by your attitude. In fact, this is making me wonder."

He paused. She turned her head. What was Connor wondering?

But she wasn't to know.

"Never mind," he said. "I'll talk about it later. You've got enough on your plate for now."

And that was the truth.

The drive to the pathologist's office passed surprisingly quickly. Cami felt ready for this in a way she hadn't before. She had no idea why. All she knew was that, in the last month or so, something had changed. Perhaps that something was her.

The pathologist's offices themselves felt like familiar territory now, and she wondered if that made it easier.

Not that much easier, she acknowledged, feeling the start of nervousness as Connor parked the car.

"Let's go," he said, his voice brisk but with a hint of compassion. She wouldn't have picked that up a couple of months ago. Connor's compassion was pretty well concealed under his tough, brusque exterior, and it had taken her a while to realize how much, and how deeply, he cared and empathized underneath it. Everyone in his team was like family to him. Although sometimes, she had to admit, it was tough love.

The scent of disinfectant and formalin hit her as they walked in, making her stomach clench. But she fought her fear and told herself this was part of the job; there was no room for nerves or nausea.

"Let's go," Connor said, leading the way. He quickly checked in with the front desk, getting the name of the doctor and the number of the room where these autopsies had been done.

Then, he handed her a mask, and they walked down the corridor, passing closed doors on either side where; Cami knew with a creepy feeling she couldn't suppress that bodies were being examined.

Connor tapped on the fourth door.

"Doc Bolton?"

Footsteps approached, and the door was opened. Cami saw a woman, gowned and masked and looking about thirty years old, standing there.

"Agent Connor here, with Cami Lark, to view the victims of the recent falls."

"Come on in, Agent Connor and Ms. Lark," she said in a friendly way. She led the way into the icy cold room, with its clean floor and clinical steel tables. Cami did her best not to look at the draped sheets, knowing what lay beneath but also knowing she'd have to soon.

She felt surprised that Doc Bolton, a woman, had made this career choice. How did she cope with it all day, Cami wondered. Surprisingly, the fact gave her a boost of encouragement. This doctor spent all day, every day, in this morgue environment. So yes, Cami told herself, she could manage a few minutes.

"Tell us about the victims," Connor asked, his voice easy. Cami fixed her eyes on the doctor's masked face.

"Well, both women died as a result of their falls. One directly, due to the impact, and one indirectly, through drowning," she said.

Connor nodded as she continued. "The first victim, Pippa Ross, seems to have slipped and fallen off the scaffolding. I wasn't on-site, but from the photos, it looks as if she was trying to cross over the deep excavation site. The scaffolding was wet from the rain. You can see there's a scrape mark on her wrist where I think she tried to grasp it with her right hand and failed."

"Was she maybe holding her phone in the other hand?" Cami surprised herself with the question. An intelligent question, while the doc was leading the way to the closest autopsy table?

"Yes, she could have been doing that," the doctor said. "It could explain why she lost her balance and fell, for sure. Being distracted by a phone, looking down..." She sighed. "Phones have caused a lot of deaths. Falls, traffic accidents. People focus on their screen, and for that moment, everything else becomes not real. If you get me."

Cami got her. She liked this doc. She nodded in understanding.

"Then, unfortunately, she hit the ground badly. She cracked her skull and would have lost consciousness immediately and probably died a minute or two later. It was an extremely serious fracture. She also had a couple of other broken bones, but without a doubt, the head injury killed her," she said sadly.

"Right," Connor said. "And her phone was found with her?"

"Yes, it was," the doctor confirmed. "It looks like it was damaged in the fall and won't provide any useful information."

"We need to check it out all the same," Connor said. "We have Cami, our tech expert, who is very good at getting information from devices."

"I'll give you the bag with the pieces," the doctor agreed. "Then, the other victim, Vicky Anderson. She was the one who climbed over the river bridge."

"And she fell into the river?" Connor asked.

"Yes. Classic death by drowning, but I'm not sure if she jumped rather than falling, as there are no signs she tried to save herself," she said. "She might have just lost her footing very suddenly."

Connor nodded grimly. "Our footage confirms that," he said.

"That fall was from a long way up, and the water was icy cold. I think what happened was that the shock of the impact and the extreme cold caused her to inhale automatically. Her lungs were flooded, and again, once that happened, she didn't stand a chance and must have died quickly."

Cami tried to keep her emotions in check as the doctor pulled back the sheet covering Pippa's body. She took a deep breath and looked, through narrowed eyes, as Connor pointed out the bruises and marks on the body.

Then, Doctor Bolton quickly showed them the other victim, Vicky, and Cami stared, with pity and compassion, into her open blue eyes, looking at the paleness of her face, thinking how terrible it was to have fallen, to have been so scared that you climbed over a railing and looked down at the dark, surging water, and considered actually letting yourself fall all that way in order to avoid – what?

Why had she done it?

"No other signs of foul play?" Connor asked.

The doctor shook her head. "Nothing unusual at all," she said. "No other injuries, no signs of anything else being wrong."

"Would you say the victims were in a heightened state of fear?"

"Yes, I would say so. The postmortem serum levels of adrenaline were higher than normal in both victims. They were definitely scared."

Cami and Connor exchanged a glance. What had scared them so badly? That was now the burning question.

At least the ordeal in the pathologist's offices had been short, and Cami felt grateful for the doctor's brisk competence and that it had not been too gory a sight to view these bodies. And now, the doc was walking to a cupboard and taking out a plastic bag.

Cami's eyes widened.

This phone really was trashed. It was little more than a heap of metal and smashed glass.

She didn't know if it would be possible to retrieve anything from it, but she took the bag from the doctor, knowing that she had to try. Hopeless as it seemed, if she could still access the basic core operating system - if any of that had remained intact - she might just learn what Pippa had been reading before she plummeted to her death.

CHAPTER SEVEN

Back in the police station, Connor watched intently as Cami bent over the ruined phone.

Carefully and patiently, with the help of a couple of basic tools, he saw that she was actually piecing together some of the phone's smashed innards. It was like watching someone solve a very complicated puzzle.

If she could do it, what would they find? Connor felt curious and hopeful as he watched. She was working with extreme competence. And her hands were steady. Connor had to admit, he was full of admiration for the way Cami had held her nerve in the autopsy room. When he compared that to the first time she'd been in a pathologist's office, he remembered how she'd been a shaking wreck for what felt like hours afterward. He'd never seen anyone look so close to throwing up for so long after leaving the autopsy room.

"Now, this goes in here," she muttered to herself, using a screwdriver to tease something almost invisible - to him - into place.

He'd thought, at the time back then, that she'd be of no use to him or the FBI, and he'd bitterly regretted what he considered to be an impulsive decision from his superior, Special Agent Fraser, to take her on.

But since then, she'd proved her mettle increasingly; she'd grown as a person, and Connor was now ready to take the next step.

He wanted to ask her if she'd consider joining the FBI and becoming a fully-fledged agent. Or else, if she'd consider joining up full-time as a non-agent tech expert who could still assist with investigations. Two offers meant two choices. He knew that guns weren't Cami's thing, and nor was she at a level of physical prowess where she'd be able to ace the training course. So maybe a tech expert would be a better choice.

The FBI was actively seeking those skills, knowing how important they were to fighting crime in today's world. That was the career choice he thought and hoped she'd pick. If she decided to pick either, of course.

There was no guarantee. She might want to go elsewhere when her year's deal was up - and if she did, he knew he'd miss her. A damned lot.

He'd talked to his girlfriend - now fiancée, about it. She was the love of Connor's life, a wise, funny woman who'd relocated to be with him and to run her interior design business from Boston. They had recently added two adopted cats to their family, and Connor couldn't remember ever having come home in the evenings with so much happiness and expectation in his heart. The fun and joy of being with her, the antics of the cats, which were a nonstop source of hilarity - and of course, the opportunity to bounce ideas off of this insightful woman who was now his life partner.

"Well, you can't force her to," his fiancée had said. "And she obviously is a very independent person."

"That she is," he agreed.

"She doesn't sound particularly money focused. So she's not going to be lured away by a startup?"

"Who knows," Connor grumbled. "They've managed to lure away most of our other tech talent."

"She doesn't sound like she's that person. She sounds like it's about the cause. And in that case, I guess the more she's exposed to it, then the more she'll realize what value she adds."

Connor had nodded, taking in her words. She was right. Cami was driven by the cause, by the idea of making a difference and helping people. And they needed people like her in the FBI, people who were passionate about the work they were doing.

"So you reckon I just keep on keeping on?"

She had quirked an eyebrow. "Your actions might convince her much louder than any words you use."

Connor hoped that his actions would be able to do that and that the FBI would get the benefit of Cami Lark's expertise for a while, at least.

There was also a complicating factor and that was not within his power to solve right now. It might affect her decision, and it wasn't even something he could safely discuss with his fiancée. At the moment, Connor was keeping Cami's predicament under wraps, although he'd advised her on what to do.

He knew she'd gotten herself involved in something, the same bigger problem that had killed Ethan. He desperately needed her to get help and guidance from an unbiased source. When that happened, and she was ready to tell him, he would do whatever it took to help her.

He watched as she inserted another piece, working with sure, nimble fingers.

And, at that moment, Connor's phone rang. He got up and moved away to answer it, not wanting to break her concentration.

It was one of the police diving teams, and he quickly picked up. A quick callback was usually a good sign. Had they found the phone?

He was in luck.

"We got it," the diver told him. "It was almost directly below the bridge marker where the victim fell from. Must have slipped straight out of her hand and down."

"I'm going to come through and get it now," Connor said. "I'll meet you by the bridge."

He turned to Cami. "They've got the other phone. I'm on my way to fetch it."

She barely looked up; she was so focused on her task.

Connor rushed out of the FBI office, glad to have a job to do while Cami worked. He got into the car and started out on the ten-minute drive that took him down to the bridge.

He didn't miss the irony, which had occurred to him earlier also, that these sites were both within ten minutes of the Boston FBI offices. Talk about misdoings occurring under the noses of law enforcement. It made him all the more eager to solve this.

Luckily traffic was on his side, and he got there ahead of time. The divers were already out of the water, waiting for him in the shelter of their car, with their wetsuits still on and their goggles pushed back.

"Chilly day for a swim," Connor greeted the diver who'd called him, a man whose quirky sense of humor he appreciated, even though, at times, it felt like gallows humor when serious crimes were being investigated.

"That's alright. We'll strip off now and suntan to warm up," the man replied, with a glance at the overcast sky, which was threatening either rain or sleet. Connor and the other diver chuckled.

"Thank you for getting this." Connor took the plastic bag from him, looking dubiously at the amount of water inside.

"I also found her purse down there, but it must have landed upside down, so there weren't any contents inside. The mud was quite thick there – we were lucky to get the phone, so I didn't look for any of the smaller possessions that might have been scattered around," he explained.

"The phone's what we need," Connor emphasized.

"Not sure if it can be resurrected from its current state," the diver acknowledged. "I've seen drier phones than this one that weren't functional again."

"I hope it can be, and thanks again," he said. "You can take the empty purse into evidence."

He took the phone in the dripping bag and headed back to his car. He wondered what tricks Cami would have up her sleeve for the best way to dry off a cell phone. They might even be useful to him and Helena because last night, one of the cats had come within a hair's breadth of knocking his phone into the bath. Or rather, a whisker's breadth. Only a lightning-fast grab had saved the situation. He grinned as he remembered how funny they'd both found it.

Then, as he headed back along the road to the FBI offices, with sleet now actually beginning to fall, his smile disappeared.

This was a serious case. Two bodies, inexplicable circumstances, and zero answers as yet.

This wet phone needed to provide some leads as to why its owner had deliberately climbed over the railing and then seemingly chosen to plunge into the icy waters far below.

He glanced at it, shivering as he drove.

Whatever it held, he knew for sure that it had caused intense fear.

And the source of that fear?

With the windshield wipers flicking, Connor gazed around at the rain-soaked streets and the dark-coated people now rushing, fast, about their business in the chilly morning.

He felt instinctively that the source of that fear was nearby here. Geographically, that was where these crimes – if they were crimes - were based. This person could be watching him drive by, even now.

And unless Connor could find out what had happened and track this person down, he feared that this would happen again.

CHAPTER EIGHT

Sleet and rain made the fingersmith's job surprisingly easy. Luckily, his fingers operated in a skillful and nimble way, even when it was very cold, even when other people had their hands swathed in gloves.

He was still able to do his job.

He glanced up as the light changed and traffic swished past. Close to the FBI offices, he wondered with a sense of amusement whether any of the drivers in those anonymous, ordinary-looking cars might be agents. There was a likelihood, of course. Always a chance.

He felt like a mouse, playing his game right outside the cat's basket. But the cat was slow and sleepy and miles behind the times, whereas the mouse was quick and agile, with lightning reflexes.

And very sharp little teeth.

He grinned at the analogy as he headed off the street and into a shopping mall, feeling the blast of hot air at the entrance cut the chill.

Now, within the more sheltered environment, people were moving with less haste. That gave him the chance to do what he needed to.

There was one, almost too easy. A woman, with her wallet literally jutting out of her coat pocket, as she dawdled along, ogling the brightly lit window of a clothing store.

He shook his head, amazed at how careless people could be, especially in such a busy mall. He decided to use this as an opportunity to teach her a lesson, to make her realize the value of being more cautious in public places.

He walked up behind on silent feet. It wasn't only a case of being quiet. It was also a case of deflection, of somehow making it evident that your energy was elsewhere. The life energy, the sense of being, that was what could attract people to you. It created a presence, a reason to be noticed.

Ever known those people who seem to turn heads and get attention wherever they go? He asked himself that question wryly as he moved softly closer. Everyone knew those people.

Their behavior, and their energy, were the opposite of what he was doing now. He was without any feeling of presence, without any awareness of himself or of her. Nothing more than a shadow. She would not notice him, and he would not notice her.

He passed by like a breath of cold winter air, and as his hand reached out and expertly removed the wallet from her pocket, it seemed not to belong to him at all.

Almost too easy. Quickly, he turned a corner and then walked briskly and purposefully to the men's room.

The wallet contained a couple of hundreds and a handful of loose change. He pocketed the money and put the rest into the trash. Perhaps some kind soul would see it and return it, and she'd get her cards back. Those were always a chore to replace. But that was where carelessness got you.

He went out again, and now that the job was done, he felt able to let his personality flare once again, chuckling in glee at his abilities and expertise, at the fact he was so much faster and smarter than anyone else. It was time to continue his shopping spree, and he'd already identified his next target. This was going to be a fun one.

He could see the shopper ahead. A young gent with a backpack on his back and two shopping bags in his hand. He was clearly on the hunt for electronic equipment. And clearly, in his bag, the man saw an iPad.

Always so useful. Nothing is more useful or easier to resell than a brand-new, unopened iPad. He didn't personally need it. He had everything he required in the communications field. But it was a little goldmine just waiting to be plundered. And he knew exactly how to go about it.

This was where the jostle would be his friend, and he had to wait for the right moment.

Perhaps there, ahead, as the young gent reached the knot of other shoppers?

Yes, that would be the perfect time.

Speeding up his walk, but not enough to attract attention, the fingersmith closed in on his target. He walked a step behind and a step to the left, his fingers already knowing the exact action and angle that they'd need in order to filch that item neatly out of the bag.

Wait, wait, not yet. Let the shoppers get a little closer. Just a little closer.

Now!

He stumbled clumsily, righting himself, bumping the young gent just enough so that he, in turn, stumbled into the oncoming group.

By then, he already had the iPad; he'd grabbed it first. He transferred it expertly to his other hand, his other side, as he gabbled out a quick apology which the young gent barely heard, as he was too busy apologizing in turn to the group he'd collided with.

Then he was gone, round a corner, slotting the item deep into the pocket of his roomy coat.

He'd gotten a couple of good targets. This had been a worthwhile expedition. But he hadn't yet identified the one person that he'd been looking out for. Experience had taught him what he needed to spot, and these targets were rare. As rare as gold. He had to find the qualities he needed, or else his resources would be wasted.

As he looked around, he saw someone who might just work.

Young - yes, they needed to be young and innocent and naive. This girl could be twenty at the most. She was looking flustered and scared as if she'd had a bad day and it was getting worse, and life was going wrong, and she felt hunted.

It was as if the fingersmith could read her mind, and he felt warm excitement flooding him.

This would be worth it. He had high hopes for her, this young, scared, flustered, and hunted target who checked all the boxes on his personal A-list.

He sidled up to her. The scared ones were jumpy, so once again, he would need to draw all his energies up inside him. To withdraw himself from the bustle of life and just be a cold breeze, moving past, indiscernible, not triggering any alarms.

He eased forward, and as he did, this time, he reached into his coat pocket, and he took out a small item.

As he passed her, he dropped it into her open purse, the movement so fast and fleeting it was as if his fingers were a blur.

He turned away casually, focusing elsewhere, withdrawing, withdrawing. And he had success.

She walked on, leaving the mall, looking warily at a man standing near the entrance and giving him a wide berth.

He felt like laughing aloud. He could have chortled and capered and danced around the mall now that this job was done and his latest target was prepared.

Oh, she was perfect. He knew that she would be a successful one.

Now, all he had to do was follow her and wait for exactly the right time.

CHAPTER NINE

Footsteps roused Cami from her intricate task of putting the broken cellphone together. She was almost done. The ruined, twisted, smashed device was assembled to the best it could be, and in a minute, they would be able to see if they could find what was on it. Assuming that it was in a state where they could even access, and bypass, its security. There was a long road ahead.

She turned her head, seeing that it was Connor, back from the store across the road with a big bag of crystal cat litter and an airtight container. That was what Cami had asked him to get to try to resuscitate the drowned phone.

Yup, cat litter was the best material available at short notice for drying out the phone. Silica was the very best but not as easy to procure. But even with the finest feline litter available, it would unfortunately take a few hours for the moisture to be drawn out of the phone sufficiently to read what was on it. If it was readable at all.

She'd already taken the drowned phone apart, removing every component from the other in order to maximize the drying-out capability.

"I brought you a big bag. Don't worry, I'll take the rest home," Connor said. "Luckily, we have two cats as of a few weeks ago. And they get through a fair amount of the stuff."

"Glad it can be put to good use," Cami agreed.

She shook a pile of the fine, transparent kitty litter into the container and added the phone's components, working carefully, piece by piece. Then, she sealed the container up.

As the hours went by, the litter would slowly draw the moisture out of the phone. She wished there was a quicker way. How she wished that blasting it with a hairdryer would achieve the same results. But it wouldn't and would potentially ruin the device, as many an impatient tech had discovered to their cost.

"I have the first one sort of pieced together," she said. "Enough to see some of what's on it. I'm going to link it up to my phone now and see what I can find. Assuming I can get in and that the security can be bypassed."

She slowly, carefully inserted the cord. The phone was so damaged that some of the components were held together by a thread. Then she plugged it into her phone.

"Let's see what we have," she muttered.

Immediately, Cami could see it wouldn't be enough. The phone was too ruined. The structure was too damaged. But she could access pieces of information, scattered fragments, even without the usual security to bypass at all. From the Sim-card itself, something was visible and was coming through.

"Messages," she said. "I can see that there were recent texts sent on this phone."

"What do they say?" Connor leaned forward. "And more importantly, who sent them?"

"The number isn't readable yet," Cami said reluctantly. "I don't know if it will be. This is like spotting a golf ball in a snowstorm. That's how scattered it is. The texts, I'm getting pieces of. It's like a puzzle."

"Are there enough to fit together?"

"That's the big question," she agreed. "At the moment, no. There are little pieces and huge gaps between them. But I'm waiting to see how much is readable, and when it's all there, then the program on my phone will put it all together. Without the program, it won't make any sense at all. But with it, we might get somewhere."

She had faith in that program. She'd tested it in the past. It was like an IT version of a brilliant puzzle solver. It could take any piece of data and look for a fit with another. It was even intelligent enough, sometimes, to be able to work out what a missing piece would include if both other fragments gave the right lead.

Poring over the coding and the logic of this program had been so worth it, Cami thought, if it would give the results they needed now.

She waited patiently, sending good vibes to the phone, telling it that it was a great machine doing a fine job. Hey, it worked. In her experience, devices responded to your attitude and thought waves. Don't knock it till you've tried it, was her stance.

And then, she had something. Another node of information was extracted from somewhere in this poor, hurt device. Now she was getting more fragments of the texts themselves. Not really enough to make any sense of. They were muddled and barely readable as yet. But what she was getting, more importantly, was some information on the caller ID from the device that had sent them.

First, one number came up, then another, then a string of three. And finally, there were seven. Triumph filled her as she looked up from the screen.

"Look here, Connor," she said. "I've gotten the last seven digits of the number that sent the texts. It might not be enough, but if we can go through the other possible codes, we could get it."

Connor nodded. "Are these the most recent texts?"

"Yes. They're the most recent, and there are several and all from the same number."

"That's excellent work." Triumph was audible in his voice. "The last seven numbers are the important ones. Going through the possible codes will be quicker. I'm going to send this straight to the expert in our tech department, who deals with the cellphone companies. They will hopefully be able to tell us the full number, and if we're lucky, we can track it."

Cami waited, feeling impatient, as Connor made the call and explained the situation. Then, they put him on hold. She passed the time by searching elsewhere on the phone. Trawling through the available information, she was getting a few more fragments.

"It seems that Vicky had a bust-up with her boyfriend a couple of weeks ago?" she said. "I'm getting something along those lines. Do you think that's correct?"

Connor nodded. "Yes, I remember that the police report from yesterday, where they interviewed her sister and housemates, mentioned that. As yet, we haven't explored it further, but we need to. A vindictive ex-boyfriend is always a factor worth following up."

"Maybe he texted her using a different phone," Cami suggested.

Connor nodded. He was still holding on, tapping his fingers on the desk impatiently. "That's a real possibility," he said. "If he did, then we need the phone number first and foremost to be able to trace it. The boyfriend himself, I believe, has left town. At any rate, the sister thought that he went home to California after the breakup. Again, this is all recent police research, and we need to check and confirm and make sure for ourselves."

At that point, the tech expert he'd been speaking to came back on the line.

"You have a location?" he asked eagerly. Then he looked disappointed, and Cami's heart plummeted.

But then, Connor looked hopeful again as he jotted down a few notes in the paper notepad he always carried with him.

He thanked the agent and hung up.

"Well, we got something," he said.

"What did we get?"

"We got the right number for sure, but the tech said it's not currently on the network and hasn't been online since yesterday, late afternoon. Probably just after Pippa died."

"So we can't track him that way?" Cami asked, feeling disappointed.

"No. I think he must have used the phone for the texting and then disposed of it. But at least he got us the shop where this phone was sold. It's a store in the center of town, and it's not a new place for us. We've had burner phones traced back to there before now. They do a lot of second-hand sales, and I suspect that some of it is off the record."

"So they won't cooperate?" Cami asked.

Connor raised an eyebrow. "They may not."

"Will this require hacking?" It sounded like it might.

"I'm not sure," Connor admitted. "We need to keep that in mind when we go there, as a possibility, because if there's information to be found, we'll need to work fast to get it. However, the problem is that off-the-record sales won't have an evidence trail linked to them because they're cash deals."

"So what do we do?" Cami was feeling nervous about this encounter. It sounded like they were going to be on the losing side of it before they'd even gotten there. But she was surprised that Connor looked more confident than she felt.

"I have some ideas," he said. "If hacking won't work, then we'll try my Plan B."

Keen to know what that might be, Cami followed him out.

CHAPTER TEN

If she'd been someone who wanted to buy a really suspect phone from a very aggressive-looking salesman, Cami thought she'd have come straight to the shop where Connor was now heading.

It was called Cell Corp, and it was a musty-smelling hole in the wall, tucked away in a corner of a dilapidated shopping mall that contained a number of empty stores, a few liquor outlets, one or two fast food kiosks, and two competing one-man barbershops that she wouldn't have gone to either of.

The shop was about eight square yards in size, and the owner occupied a full square yard of that space. He was an enormous man, big-shouldered, with a broad face, a huge pot belly, and glowering brows. Behind him, on the wall hangers and shelves, were ranks of phones. The shop was lined with more shelves containing dusty accessories.

Connor approached the counter with his badge visible. The man's expression barely changed.

"What do you want?" he grunted.

"We're investigating a possible crime," Connor explained. "We see that you sold a phone with this number in the past few weeks. Can you give me the buyer's details?"

He showed the man the printed page on which the phone's number appeared.

The man stared down at it.

"You got a warrant?"

"Not yet," Connor said.

"We don't give out customer information without a warrant. It's privileged, you know. You guys, do you think you can just barge in and call the shots in my shop? You're the second set of cops I've kicked out of here in as many weeks. People value their privacy, and that's why I get business."

Cami could already see there was going to be little opportunity to hack into these systems. For a start, this really did seem like a place where cash deals were done and records were skimpy. And in addition, she couldn't see any security cameras that would help her. There was one at the door. That wouldn't help them if they didn't know exactly what time the customer who bought that particular phone had come in. If someone had walked in, paid cash, and left with the phone, they wouldn't know who he was or when he'd bought it, and they couldn't run all the footage hoping to find one unknown person.

She guessed that Connor had concluded the same. This was an aggressive, obstructive man, and he ran a cash business hands-on. The only way they were going to get information out of him was by being clever about it.

And Cami acknowledged that Connor was far better at getting that side of things than she was. She had zero chance. Connor, on the other hand, had more of a chance.

"I guess you run a good, fair business here," he said.

The man shrugged. "I'd do better if the mall was busier."

"It's not a seasonal thing? Winter, you know?"

Cami listened, feeling intrigued, realizing that this was Connor's Plan B in action. Much more subtle than she'd expected.

"Yeah, it's always quieter in winter. But the mall is not looking after us. Look at it! It's a dump! And what are they doing? Are they refurbishing it? Nope, they're planning to build a brand new one down the road."

"I wish I could speak to a few people in city planning," Connor agreed, in tones that sounded heartfelt. And now, Cami could see the owner nodding. Now, it was as if he and Connor were on the same side. She genuinely didn't know how he'd achieved that with only a couple of minutes of empathetic conversation. But surprisingly, he had.

"You find things safe here? Or is there some theft?" he asked.

"We need more policing here, that's for sure," the store owner grumbled.

"I know. Name of the game. We're under-resourced here. Funny thing, though." Cami realized that Connor had an instinct and was following it. "I was wondering if this phone might have come up on your stolen list. As I was told, the card was activated in a roundabout way. Not at the time of purchase, but sometime after that."

"I guess I could look that up," the owner said. Grudgingly, but he said it at least. Through his chit-chat, Connor had gotten him to open up to the extent where he was at least prepared to go into the records.

Now, if the phone wasn't stolen, maybe they'd get a name. But Cami realized, with an uneasy feeling, that it might well be stolen. Especially if the card had been activated in an unusual way.

43

"We don't get much theft here, usually. That's why I don't bother with an internal camera," the man said. "Just the one at the door, so my insurance is happy. But I must say, the other day, we did have someone come in who walked out with a couple of phones. And I've been hearing from other store owners that they've had similar issues. Recent phone thefts. "

"Could be our man," Connor agreed.

"Let me have a look."

Now, the man was looking through a well-thumbed hardcover journal, going back through the records.

"Yeah," he said. "Hate to break it to you, but that number was one of the two stolen devices. I don't know how the hell he did it. He was like a normal customer, browsing around. I guess the hood should have clued me in."

"So he had a hood?"

"Yeah. But I was distracted; I was on a call, I was just watching him, and he walked out. I never even got a good look at his face. I never would have thought he'd have stolen anything. He was very good because I'm sharp."

"What about his clothing? Build?"

"Average," the man said. "Average height, not a big man, and I didn't get a good look at his face. He stole two phones, I see. I will give you the other number, just in case, for the good it'll do." He jotted it down on Connor's page.

"I'll have a word with the local police," Connor said. "See what they can do."

"Hope you find him," the man said.

"And I hope your business picks up and that we find this thief so you can carry on doing your business. You take care," Connor said.

They left the shop, with Cami feeling blindsided by Connor's skillful expertise. He was such a people person. They didn't have a whole lot of information, but at least they had some. They knew these phones had been stolen, and it was by someone who was of average height and build, a skillful thief who'd kept his face hidden.

And now, Cami guessed that he must be using these phones as burners. Messaging one victim and then discarding the phone so it couldn't be traced back to him. It was a perfect cutoff loop. She was sure that they'd find Vicky and Pippa had been messaged from different devices.

"You think it could be the ex-boyfriend?" Cami asked as soon as they had left the store.

Connor shook his head. "The ex-boyfriend was a big guy, over six foot, from what the sister said. This sounds like a different person. But what I am wondering is whether either of these victims might have known this man or seen him before."

"You mean?" Cami asked. As they strode back through the dilapidated mall, she was battling to work out what Connor meant. She thought she knew, but yet she wasn't sure.

"I mean, maybe he was taking his time with them. Maybe he stalked them for a while, while he was messaging them or even before he started. And if we're lucky, they might have mentioned that to someone."

CHAPTER ELEVEN

It was time to look into the backgrounds of these two victims and see if anything, or anyone, might be lurking there. Cami thought it was a very likely theory that this stalker had been targeting them for a while. He sounded like the type of creepy guy who would do just that.

Pippa Ross was the closer of the two victims in terms of her location. While Connor drove to her house, he got on the phone to the local police station in her area of Boston. If she'd had trouble, this was where it would have been reported.

"Agent Connor here. I'm looking to see if a recent victim of death by misadventure, Pippa Ross, had filed any reports of harassment, stalking, or anything of the kind?" Glancing down while he was stopped at a light, he read out her address details and the case number for her death.

"Hold on, and I'll check it up," the woman on the other end of the phone said.

After a few moments, the woman on the phone came back on the line. "I'm sorry, Agent Connor, but we don't have any reports on file from Pippa Ross. I've gone back two years. You want me to go further?"

"Not necessary, thanks," Connor said.

He hung up and concentrated on getting them to Pippa's neighborhood fast.

As he twisted and turned his way through a series of back streets, Cami saw that Pippa had lived in a rather rundown area of Boston that might be described as a shabby neighborhood or else as eclectic chic, depending on who you were and whether you liked the sense of character that wear and tear created.

Glancing at Connor's case notes, she saw that Pippa had lived alone on the first floor of a two-story building. And on the corner, so she only had one neighbor.

When they got out of the car, Cami saw that the small apartment which she'd rented was now locked up tight, with curtains drawn, and dark. But someone had placed a bunch of flowers on the doormat outside the front door, a touching sight.

Connor glanced at the case notes once again before he got out.

"Pippa's closest relative lives in Pittsfield, all the way on the other side of Massachusetts," he said. "So she was alone here. She had no boyfriend but a few work colleagues in the clothing factory where she worked. If the neighbor doesn't know anything, then the factory could be our next stop. The police haven't been there yet, as it was ruled to be a death by misadventure, and they weren't aware of any other factors."

He walked up to the next-door apartment and tapped on the door.

After a few moments, the neighbor answered the door. She was a woman in her sixties, with sharp blue eyes and closely cropped hair dyed a bright, striking red. Cami immediately liked that rebellious touch. She hoped this woman might know more.

Her eyes widened when she saw the FBI on her doorstep.

"Morning, ma'am. I'm Agent Connor, and this is my colleague, Cami Lark," Connor said. "We're investigating the death of Pippa Ross, and we were wondering if you knew anything about her. If she'd had any difficulties, any trouble with anyone recently?"

"I'm Debbie Higgs," the woman said. "I knew Pippa quite well. She moved in two years ago." She paused, looking thoughtful. "I guess we used to chat a couple of times a week, usually on our doorstep, when we were both going in or out."

"Did she ever mention anything about feeling unsafe or perhaps even being stalked or harassed?" Connor asked.

The neighbor shook her head. "No, I never heard her complain about anything like that." She was silent for a while. "You know, it wouldn't have surprised me if she had, though."

"Why's that?" Connor asked, as Cami's ears pricked up. Were they on the right track here?

"She was a very sensitive young woman. She was very easily upset and very quick to believe the world was against her. She was - well, easily led, I guess you could say. Not to speak badly of her at all, and I'm deeply upset by what happened, but she was one of those young women who's easily going to end up believing that the world is against her. I picked that up in a few of our conversations. So I guess she could have thought someone was following her. Or maybe she did have a stalker, and I was the one who was trying to convince her she was wrong," she added thoughtfully.

Now that was very interesting, Cami thought.

"But you never got any actual proof? Did you see anyone outside?" Connor asked.

She shook her head. "Pippa kept to herself. She had a quiet life. Her job took up a lot of her time. She worked very long shifts, and I don't think she was paid very well. She used to try to do a lot of overtime. She'd occasionally have friends around or go out, but it was always quiet. She was a good neighbor and considerate."

"Was she friends with Vicky Anderson?" Connor showed the woman a photo of the second victim.

She shook her head. "I don't recall seeing that woman here. She might have been, but I don't remember it."

"Thank you very much," Connor said.

Armed with this sketchy but interesting information, they turned away.

"Let's head to Pippa's work," Connor decided. "We're getting a picture of her now, but I'd like to fully rule out that there was any trouble in her life. At the moment, it's fifty-fifty whether there really was or whether she just thought so."

They climbed back into the car, and Connor wove his way through the streets, heading out of this eclectic and likable neighborhood - the color of that neighbor's hair had definitely swayed Cami to that side of the fence - and into a light industrial area a few miles away.

"She worked at Fabric Fusion," Connor said, checking the notes, and the map, as he headed down the second of two rows of small warehouses.

There, ahead, was the green and pink sign on top of one of the large double doors.

They parked in the crowded lot nearby and walked over to the factory, where Cami could already hear the noise of conversation, and soft music, coming from inside.

The brightly lit interior was laid out in three rows of tables, with sewing machines and overlockers, mannequins and drapes of fabric, and four seamstresses busy at work.

The closest seamstress, a dark-haired woman who looked about Pippa's age, hurried over to the door immediately, setting down the bright green dress she'd been working on. A moment later, the conversation and the music hushed. All eyes were on them.

"FBI," Connor introduced them briefly, showing his ID. "We're following up on Pippa's death."

Somber nods all around.

"It's so tragic," the closest woman said, brushing her hand nervously over the half-finished dress.

"She received some messages before her death, and we're trying to find out more about them. Do you know if she had any problems, any harassment or stalkers?"

They all exchanged glances.

"Not really," the closest woman said. "But she was - well, she was a fearful personality. She often worried that something was wrong."

"We spent a lot of time reassuring her," one of the others said. "She used to think, sometimes, that she was being followed and that people were – well, that the world was a dangerous place, and people were too, and she was likely to be a target."

"She definitely had a very high awareness of stranger danger," one of the others said.

"But there was never anything concrete?"

"Absolutely not. We have cameras outside here, and they would have picked up if anyone was nearby," the closest woman said. "We used to check the footage often to reassure her and make sure she knew she was safe here. And if we worked late, one of us would always walk her to her car. I did that often, but I never saw anything or felt that anything was wrong."

Again, Connor asked if Pippa had known Vicky, and this time the headshakes were more decisive.

They thanked the team and turned away.

It was time to head to Vicky's neighborhood now, and Cami felt intrigued by what she'd picked up so far.

Pippa hadn't been stalked, but she had been fearful.

Was that her nature?

Had Vicky picked up on something subtle but dangerous that was really happening in her life? And if so, did someone close to her know about this secret?

CHAPTER TWELVE

Was this a case of a stalker having slowly closed in on his victims? Listening to the accounts of Pippa's coworkers and neighbors, Cami still wasn't sure. There hadn't been anything concrete to pick up, and nobody had seen anything. But Vicky had lived in a house-share environment, and Cami felt hopeful that having friendly people living closer by might make this easier to figure out.

"After all," she said thoughtfully, "someone who's feeling paranoid and believes they're being followed might not necessarily go to the police straight away. They might doubt themselves."

"Yes, that's true," Connor agreed as they approached the front door.

"Pippa seems like the kind of person who would do that. Doubt herself, I mean," Cami said. "Maybe Vicky was a similar person?"

After all, they already knew that Vicky had experienced problems in her life. Had they been compounded by the presence of a stalker? Connor had called the local police on the way, just as he'd done before arriving at Pippa's house. But there were no reports from Vicky herself.

Connor knocked on the door of the double-story home, which was a little further out of town and in an area where students, young families, and retirees seemed to live in friendly convergence.

A young man in his early twenties, with spiky dark hair and wearing a waterproof jacket over his running gear, answered the door. He looked surprised to see the FBI standing on his doorstep.

"Good afternoon, sir," Connor said, showing his badge. "We're investigating the death of Vicky Anderson. We'd like to ask you and the other housemates some questions, if that's okay?"

He looked dubious. "Two of them aren't in. Elena is away on a college trip, and Simone's at work. So it's just me and Grace. I'm Marcus. Can you speak to us? I'll gladly help. But I thought it was just an accident?"

"We always have to investigate every death thoroughly in case there are any other factors in play," Connor explained. "In this case, there was a similar death a couple of days apart. So it's on our radar, and we need to work out what happened."

"Vicky never seemed like a suicidal person at all," Marcus admitted. "And she also didn't strike me as a person who'd take a wild dare."

"You and Grace will be very helpful in giving us more details," Connor said. Marcus stepped aside, and Cami walked into the cluttered and slightly messy home behind Connor.

"Grace! Grace, the police are here. I mean, the FBI! Can you come downstairs?" Marcus called as he led the way into the living room. They sat down - Connor and Cami side by side on a two-seater couch and Marcus on a wicker chair in the corner. That left a scuffed but comfortable-looking armchair for Grace - who hurried downstairs. Dressed in faded jeans and a sweater, with ink stains on her hand and eyeglasses on her face, she looked at Cami as if she'd been studying. She knew that thousand-yard stare that meant someone had been ripped away from their books.

"We want to know if Vicky experienced anything unusual or worrying in the past few weeks," Connor said. "Anyone following her, any stalker, anything like that."

The two housemates exchanged a shocked glance.

"You think something like that was going on in her life?" Marcus asked. "That's terrible. I must say I never heard her complain, but I didn't have such a close friendship with her."

"I did," Grace said. She was fidgeting and looking uneasy. Looking at her more closely, Cami thought for sure that she might have something important to say.

"Please, explain?" Connor invited.

"Well, I don't want to sound paranoid," Grace said hesitantly.

"Any information will help us a lot. I'll be glad if you can share it," Connor invited.

"I was actually the one who thought she might have a stalker. I mentioned it to Vicky, and of course, she got really worried because she was that type of person. You know, highly strung. Things upset her. But a week or so ago, I was sure there was someone who was lurking around and trying to look in through the downstairs bedroom window - which is her room. I never caught him in the act, though, but I tried when I saw him."

"Can you describe him?"

"He was about Marcus's height but bigger. You know, a more solid build. I think he had brown hair."

"And did you get any other details? A car license plate, anything of that kind?"

To Cami's surprise, Grace nodded.

"Sort of," she said. "I tried to get a picture of the license plate. I saw him getting into a white car down the road. But unfortunately, the photo was totally blurry. You know, I was so rushed. So I didn't go to the police with it, because what could they do with a useless photo? And then, I guess, I convinced myself I'd probably just imagined it all anyway."

Cami exchanged a glance with Connor. That blurry photo might be a strong lead.

"Can you show me the photo?" she asked. "In fact, can you forward it to me by email?" That was likely to give her a better-quality image to work from.

Grace took out her phone, looking excited to be helping the police. She sent the photo, and a few moments later, it pinged into Cami's inbox.

"Anything else you noticed, anything more you want to mention?" Connor checked.

The two shook their heads.

"Did Vicky know a woman called Pippa?" Connor tried. "This is what she looks like."

More headshakes as he showed Pippa's photo to them.

"What about her boyfriend? Tell me about him?" Connor asked.

Grace took a deep breath.

"Vicky was very upset when he broke up with her, but he said his job meant he was away too often, and he just couldn't commit, and he wanted to move to California because more of his driving jobs were based there. He called last night. He'd heard about this and was very upset. He wanted to know if there was anything he could do. I think he felt responsible, you know, after the breakup. That maybe he'd somehow caused this. But how could he? He was busy moving someone's household contents across the country. I think he said he was in Ohio when this had happened."

Driving across a number of states effectively ruled the boyfriend out, and Cami knew that Connor would now have finally cleared him.

"How about the other housemates?" Connor then asked. "Do you know if they saw anything unusual, anything similar to what you have done?"

More headshakes. "Nobody spoke about a stalker. I think I was the only one to see that guy, although when I mentioned it, Becky also said she thought she saw him, too. But she didn't take any photos. It was more a glimpse."

Connor thanked the two housemates. It looked like there was no more information to be gained, but they had some very useful pointers. There had been an actual stalker, and he'd been peering into Vicky's window.

Cami looked around carefully when they were outside, but there were no street cameras nearby. There was no way of getting a clearer image that they had - and they'd been lucky to get it at all.

Now to see if her software could make a head or tail of the extremely blurry photo.

Cami started working on it as soon as she was in the car. It was going to be a challenge, for sure. Not only was it out of focus, but Grace's photography skills had not even managed to get the entire plate in the frame. There was only the last part of the number.

"You think you can get something fast? Or will it take long?" Connor asked.

"If it works, I'll get something within a few minutes," Cami said, watching her software working on the blurred and pixellated image.

"In that case, I'll stay right here in the car. Because if you can get enough of that for us to ID the plate, we're going straight there."

Straight to the stalker.

Cami suppressed a shiver as she worked, hoping that her software would manage to do the job. A creepy guy like that, who'd been peering through windows, was exactly the person she imagined had somehow been responsible for triggering these women to do what they'd done.

Finally, after what felt like an eternity, the software flashed up a result, and Cami quickly looked at what it had found.

"Here you go," she said to Connor. "The last three digits are definite. The one before that is possible."

Connor nodded, his eyes narrowed. "Given that it's most likely a Massachusetts plate, I'm going to call it in. If it is local, they'll be able to give us a match for it. Good work there."

He got on the phone straight away, reading out the available digits.

"Assuming it's a plate from this state, do we have an owner ID for it?" he asked.

"Hold on one sec," Cami heard the tinny background voice of the man on the other side of the line. "I'm taking a look."

There was a pause.

"Okay. The vehicle is a white Mazda sedan, and the owner is Austin Rix."

"You got an address?"

"I sure do," he said. "Austin Rix's address is in Boston, on the western side. I'm going to send it to you now. If you want other details, he's a twenty-five-year-old male. I'll send what I have through."

"Any previous history of stalking?" Connor asked the policeman.

Another pause.

"No. I can't see any record, but our system is updating. So if he had any arrests in the past three months, that information wouldn't be available. As soon as it's updated, if there's anything, I'll call you back."

"Thanks," Connor said.

He started the car, and Cami glanced at the phone. There was the blurry ID photo of Austin Rix, together with his address details, date of birth, and other information.

She felt a mixture of fear and excitement as she thought she might be looking at the picture of the stalker who'd somehow triggered a situation where two women had fallen to their death.

And in a few more minutes, they might be face-to-face with the killer.

CHAPTER THIRTEEN

This was where Austin Rix lived? When Connor pulled up outside his registered address, at 2 Baytree Drive, Cami had to admit it didn't seem like the right place for a stalker to reside. Not that she knew much about stalkers, but she'd had other pictures in her mind.

This home was a modern-looking, compact home, part of a new development, with a concrete pathway leading to the front door, big windows, and some steel detail near the roof.

"Wonder if he's home?" Connor asked himself as he knocked on the gray-painted front door.

Cami waited expectantly, staying a step behind Connor, looking out for this man who'd been seen so fleetingly by Vicky's housemate. Who was he? And what powers, or hold, had he managed to gain over the two women that both had died in such extreme ways while suffering such fear? She wished she'd been able to read more of the messages on Pippa's phone. The fragments that had been retrievable hadn't said nearly enough. Getting a full record of the messages would surely help them match up the sender's writing style with who he really was. And also the threats might contain specifics, too.

But maybe the answers would be found here regardless.

After a few moments, she heard footsteps and tensed.

The door opened, and a man who looked about twenty-five, with messy brown hair and a worried expression, appeared. He looked like the photo Cami had seen on her phone, although he looked less solid in real life and definitely more wary.

"Austin Rix?" Connor asked.

"That - er - that's me," he said. He didn't sound too sure about it, Cami thought. His gaze was darting around, taking in Connor's appearance and size, looking at Cami, and then focusing beyond.

"We have a few questions for you in connection with a case," Connor said.

"A case? I don't think I'm a criminal." Austin gave a braying, snorting laugh and then looked embarrassed about it, his face flushing pink.

"We're not saying you are, Mr. Rix," Connor said. "But we do need to ask you a couple of questions for clarification."

"What's this about?" Now there was a stubborn set to his jaw. After the shock of seeing the FBI at his door, he was quickly regrouping, Cami saw.

"It's in connection with the recent deaths of two women in the area," Connor said, his tone serious.

Austin's eyes widened, and he took a step back. "I don't know anything about that."

Connor took the opportunity to take a step forward. Now his foot was over the threshold, and Austin would find it a lot harder to the door it in his face. Cami had seen that Connor was very good at doing these small and subtle actions that ended up positioning him more strategically. It was like a game of chess, she thought.

"Do you know a woman called Vicky Anderson?" Connor asked.

Cami saw Austin's face twitch.

"Vicky?" he blurted out. Then, in a different and more restrained tone, "Vicky, who did you say?"

"Can we come in, please?" Connor said. "Let's talk about this inside. It's cold out."

Austin, who was wearing a long-sleeved, but light-looking top, was also looking cold as the wind gusted past them and into the small hallway.

"Okay," he said reluctantly.

He stepped back and gestured for them to enter. The house was sparsely furnished, with clean lines and a minimalist feel. The living room door was ahead. There, Cami noted a few books on a shelf, an empty pizza box, and a laptop open on the coffee table with a half-finished cup of coffee beside it. Like the outside of the house, the inside seemed very ordinary.

"We understand you were seen near Vicky's home a couple of days ago," Connor said as they sat down on the black leather couch.

"Now, Austin looked at him with a careful expression.

"I don't recall that," he said. "What's the address?"

Connor read it out, and Austin shook his head.

"Can't say I've been there," he said.

He was lying, and Cami felt frustrated about it. While Connor was plowing on with the questions, she turned to her phone, wondering if it would be possible to hack into his wifi. That might give her a lead to his phone, and that, in turn, might mean they made some progress here.

She ran her program, noting that this wifi looked to have been professionally set up and that the password might not be the easiest to crack.

Unless he'd made it easier to remember, as so many people did? And how would he have done that?

Using his date of birth? Which she just happened to have right in front of her because it was part of the record that the police had sent them.

Feeling as if it was worth a try, Cami directed her brute-force program to begin with every possible version of the birth date. While it went to work, she tuned in again to the conversation.

Now, Austin was getting more aggressive. He still wasn't cooperating, and he was being stubborn.

"I'm not willing to tell the police all about my life and my doings! Haven't you guys ever heard of privacy? I'm an innocent person. I mean, I'm a night manager for a cleaning company. I have a normal job. I'm a normal guy."

That explained why he wasn't at work now, Cami thought. Because his job meant he was working at night. But that gave him the whole day to track down potential victims. A night manager could easily have been involved in these women's deaths because he would have had time in the day to stalk and taunt and do whatever he had done.

She glanced down and saw, to her relief, that her hunch had worked. She was in. She'd gotten onto his wifi. His phone was connected to it, and his computer, too. The phone would be a better source of information, but it was slower to get into. The computer would be faster.

Cami unobtrusively moved her fingers over her phone's screen, deciding to go for the computer first. He might have some phone apps linked up to it, and then she'd be able to see them faster.

As she navigated through Austin's computer, she saw that he had several dating apps downloaded. She took a look into a couple of them, wondering if any of them might hold a clue to his involvement in the deaths of the two women.

He didn't seem to be very good at dating, that she saw. He was a serial messenger. He liked to message women back and forth in a flirty way, but then when it came to the actual dating, he backed off. Or else, by the time he got the courage to ask them out, they did.

Here! Here was something.

Here was Vicky. Cami's eyes widened. Vicky had been on the dating site. Recently, too. It looked like she'd done it after her breakup. That would have been on the rebound, which was understandable. Maybe he'd been waiting, searching for someone like her. And he'd clicked on her profile. And he'd messaged her.

They'd exchanged a few messages. Vicky had told him where she worked. She hadn't said where she'd lived – at any rate, that information wasn't in the messages she could see, but he might easily have found that out. He could even have followed her home.

He'd asked if he could meet her. But then, she'd backed off. She'd said she'd bust up with her boyfriend too recently and that she'd rushed into this and she needed some space. She'd been the one to say no. He hadn't taken no for an answer, though, had he?

Unfortunately, she couldn't get onto his phone's private messaging. So outside of the site, she couldn't see if Austin had sent Vicky any texts personally. But everything was pointing to it since he knew a fair amount about her.

Cami cleared her throat. It was time to get onto the questions she wanted to ask Austin directly. The ones she hoped might shock him into giving them the truth and put a stop to this defiant parrying.

"Tell me," she said when there was a gap in Connor's questions. "The dating app, Boston Buzz. Are you on it?"

He stared at her, gaping in shock.

"I - yeah, I am. Yeah. How did you know?"

Cami thought it wiser not to admit that she'd just been prying into his computer.

"I've done some research into it. It's an easy site to research if you're a hacker, which I am."

His eyes were widening now as she continued. "I was able to see a few of the matches that some people made. And I noticed that you matched up with Vicky a while ago," she said.

Austin was now staring at her as if he was shell-shocked.

"How did you know that?" he asked in a high, confused tone. Then, anger followed. "This is, like, my personal life! You have no right to pry into it! That's unacceptable," he ranted.

"Why don't you just tell us what happened between the two of you?" Cami asked. "Did you stalk her? Did you try to meet her? Did you go and see what she looked like in person? Did you message her on your phone? Why is privacy such a big issue for you? What are you hiding?"

He stared at her, and the anger in his face slowly ebbed.

"I guess - well, I guess I wanted to find out why she didn't want to meet. I got rather obsessed by it. I'm so bad at asking women out. And then, one of the few times I do, she suddenly backs off and says no?" He shook his head angrily. "I guess I was very embarrassed about it. And I wanted to see if she was with someone else if that was the reason, so I knew if it would be okay to try again at some stage. So yeah, I went and spied on her, and then I felt very bad."

"Because of her privacy?" Connor asked, and he nodded, shamefaced.

"Because yeah, I went into their yard, I went onto private property, I even tried to look through the windows to see which was her room – she'd said she had a view of the road, so I thought I knew. But then I thought her housemate saw me, so I quickly left. I felt so bad about all of it. I can't believe I behaved that way. What an idiot. Why couldn't I take no for an answer?"

His face was flushing crimson, and Cami found that she did believe him. His story, and his emotions, rang true to her. But Connor was harder to convince.

"Your movements yesterday, early evening? Say, from four p.m.? Can you tell me where you were?"

That timeframe was when Pippa Ross had received the messages and fallen to her death.

He nodded. "Yesterday early evening, I was at a dentist's appointment. My appointment was at four, but the doc was running late, so I went in at four thirty, finished up at half past five, and then went straight on to work at six."

"Can you confirm that? And also, show me the texts on your phone. I want to see your activity from yesterday afternoon."

Cami knew that if he could do that, he was cleared. If Austin had been in the dentist's waiting room and then in the chair, he was cleared.

He showed Connor his phone.

Cami watched Connor nod. And she knew, just like that, their suspect was no longer possible. He had an alibi.

As they stood up, her thoughts went back to Vicky's phone, packed away in the cat litter.

It was evening now, and the phone had been there a few hours.

"I want to go back to that water-damaged phone," she said. "There's a chance we could get information off it now, and if so, we might have a new lead."

CHAPTER FOURTEEN

The fingersmith was happy. So very happy. Because this woman was exactly who he'd thought she was. And he'd begun the process of reeling her in.

Reeling her in on his line until she was in his power and at his mercy.

She was someone who always obsessively read texts the minute they landed. That boded well; he knew from experience.

"I'm going to have a date with you, my sweetheart. It's coming up soon. I'm already in your mind. You might find that strange, but I have a very special ability that the dark powers have gifted me. Are you ready for me to live with you in your head?" he sent, smiling to himself. He was holed up in a cafe, in the warmth, with a cup of coffee in front of him.

But he knew where she was; he knew exactly where. It might even be fun to take a walk past there later. That would add a whole new layer of fun to this pursuit, and it would also mean that he could include some important detail in his messages to her. Detail that would mean that she took the messages more seriously because she truly thought he was there.

She'd read the text. Nothing back, of course. Why would there be? His targets never responded, but they read. They read, and they reacted. And the reactions were what brought him joy. Especially when they broke. That was wonderful. It was like seeing prey flushed out of hiding and on the run, knowing the outcome would be destructive or even deadly.

The thought of her, wide-eyed with fear and vulnerability, sent a shiver down his spine.

That was the pattern, it was how it went, and oh, he loved it.

"Tell me what buildings you like," he wrote. *"Do you like that church on the corner, near to where you are now? That's a pretty building, isn't it? I can see it, just like you. I'm walking alongside you because you let me into your mind."*

He was pleased that a quick glance at the map had offered that information so authentic. It was all about the detail, after all.

More shocked silence. She wasn't saying a thing in reply now.

"Yes, I feel that you and I could have a moment there," he said. *"Although it's a bit early for wedding bells, but who knows? Other things happen in churches, don't they? Those are the things I enjoy more, actually."*

He wondered if she'd immediately think of funerals because that was where he wanted her thoughts to go. That way. To darkness and death, building a sense of threat. A sense that he already owned her.

"Oh, I see you're past the church now. So we missed the chance to get married. But I'm with you all the same. Invisible and present. Just now, I'll make myself known to you."

Her location had been in the same place for a while now. He guessed, looking closely at where she was standing, off the street, that she must be home. He checked it on the map, seeing it was an area of small houses and cramped apartment blocks. It was likely she lived there, a short walk from the church. That was good. Now he knew he could start researching all the landmarks that were in the neighborhood. It would feel exactly as if he was haunting her. He could bring so much intimacy to the texts that way. He would be burrowing down into her mind and finding all the trigger points. And he was good at it. He had a natural talent for doing it.

The fingersmith's lips stretched wide into a cruel, humorless smile at the thought.

Then, remembering that he was sitting in a public place, he double-checked that his phone's location was set to private and that nobody could see what he was writing - not in a mirror, not in a camera, not in a window. It was essential that he stay anonymous. He didn't want to be found out and have the police stop his fun.

He was too clever for the police, but being clever meant thinking ahead. Only stupid people didn't do that.

Having done a quick privacy check, he returned to the messaging. This time he would compose one that talked about what she'd been wearing. That dove gray jacket. The hem had been loose on one side. That would be a very handy thing to point out. She'd be scared, especially if he said he'd just noticed it.

That might flip the switch on its own.

He began typing the words, choosing them carefully for maximum effect.

But then, his eyebrows shot up. He'd received an incoming text that had arrived while he was busy typing out his message to her.

"This is Bert, Bianca's dad. I have her phone. I've seen your texts, you creep. Stop upsetting my daughter. If you text her again, I'm taking this straight to the police. And in the meantime, I'm blocking you."

He felt himself go red, felt his breath come fast as the number went opaque. He'd been blocked. Stopped in his tracks. The unexpected had happened, and an angry father had intervened and spoiled the beauty of the hunt.

How dare that man call him a creep? How he wished he could target him, turn him into a quivering, terrified wreck that would be sorry for what he'd done. But he knew it would not work. He could text the dad from here to eternity, and the dad would not be vulnerable to the messages, and worst of all, he'd ripped his daughter away. Now, his fun and his chances were over; his hopes were dashed.

He let the fury fill him, let it slowly ebb, reminded himself that not every chase was successful and nor could it be. He had a rate of about one success for every two failures so far. For some weird reason, the women themselves seldom blocked him if he created enough of a sense of fear early on. But their friends and family, who were less susceptible, often made them do just that. He'd had a similar message two days ago.

He wanted to improve on his hit rate, of course, but you couldn't account for wild cards like this. Luckily he had a few spare phones. He could start again with a new one. Time to turn this one off now, for good.

He'd throw it away later, when he left the coffee shop, after wiping it down.

The mall was busy; the restaurants were filling up, the late-night shops were making a good trade, and people were flocking to the movies. He'd find someone else, and he knew who to look for. The people who weren't in the mall to have fun but who were there to do some quick shopping, who looked uneasy and worried, in a rush, who seemed like they'd be the kind of person to live alone.

It was difficult to find them, but when the fingersmith saw them, he knew them with a cold certainty.

And they were out there, those little gems, those beautiful women who would read his texts, and the tone and the content would create a sense of terror in them so extreme that logical thought could not prevail.

Not all women had a protective father in their corner. Most didn't. He'd just been unlucky, and that meant his luck was due to turn.

He downed his coffee, stood up, and pocketed the burner phone, as well as his own personal device. Left a ten-dollar note on the plate. Stolen money, he could get more if he needed to. He always tipped well, but not too well, because wait staff noticed people who didn't tip at all, and he didn't want to be noticed. It was essential for his purposes that he stayed invisible.

Now, to continue the hunt.

The late-night grocery store at the far end of the mall might be his best bet to attract a new woman. If he got exactly the right one, he could move fast. If she was on the way home, he could start texting her straight away.

His luck might turn tonight after all, and if it didn't, then he was a patient man. He could wait until tomorrow morning. After all, when it happened, it was always worth the wait.

With renewed purpose, walking faster, the fingersmith strode to the late-night grocery store.

CHAPTER FIFTEEN

"I reckon we try Vicky's phone now," Cami said to Connor as soon as they were back in the car. "If it's dried out enough, we could get some more information off it tonight. If not, we put it back until tomorrow morning."

"It can't damage it worse if you take it out early?" Connor asked.

"Nope. It'll either work or it won't," Cami said confidently, reassured by years of experience and many memories of tinkering with damaged phones. She was one of the best in terms of technical expertise. Everyone at college wanted Cami to fix their broken or drowned phone. She personally thought it was because she had a subtle touch and a fair amount of patience.

Not all the time, and not often with human beings, but with devices.

Connor nodded, and they swung in the direction of the FBI building. Again, Cami noted how close it was. This was an easy drive back. There hadn't yet been a suspect or a victim that had taken them far out of town.

Connor checked the time as he parked outside the building.

"Seven-thirty p.m.," he said in surprise. "That was a busy day."

"I hope we get a lead," Cami said. All she could think was that it had been a wasted day. They'd gotten some information but no suspect. The killer was out there, and it was making her very nervous that they didn't know who he was.

Connor nodded in agreement. "Me too. Let's hope the phone has something for us."

Cami headed into the building, knowing that it would have a more muted feel after hours. A lot of the agents had gone home; the office staff had clocked out for the day. It was always quieter now, but to her, it never felt as if this building was sleeping. She doubted it ever did. With so many floors of agents and so many serious crimes, she was sure that at any given hour on any given day, there'd be someone inside.

Who, in this huge FBI office, had been the one involved in Ethan's killing? Who had known that she'd left Liam a message?

She was sure it was someone here. It sounded as if Ethan had been looking at internal issues, not at anything outside the FBI.

Putting the thought out of her mind, Cami headed into Connor's office.

She could see straight away that there was a mist of condensation on the inside of the container. That was good. Water that was on the inside of the container was water that was no longer in the phone's mechanism.

Cami carefully opened the container and removed the phone, shaking it free from the litter, inspecting it closely. Then she carefully put all the components back together again, and she turned it on.

"Partial success," she said. It was working. Maybe not fully, and the screen was very water damaged, but she was getting power, and that meant, if she could get past the security, she'd be able to see some of what was there.

Time to let her software run and see if it was possible to access this phone's messages.

She heard footsteps behind her and swung around, her heart suddenly speeding up, realizing that Connor hadn't come in with her. Who was here? Who was coming in when she was on her own?

But it was Connor, to her relief. He was walking in with two packages of food and two sodas.

"I thought now might be a good chance to have some dinner while your software works," he said.

"That sounds wonderful."

Cami felt grateful for Connor's concern. Never once when she'd been on a case with him had she gone hungry. He'd always taken the time to grab some food for both of them. This time he'd chosen spicy chicken burgers. Just what she needed after a long day.

While her phone communicated, slowly and tortuously, with the water-damaged phone, Cami bit into her burger, devouring it hungrily.

Maybe it was the result of all that food inside her, feeding her brain these much-needed calories, but Cami suddenly had an idea.

Liam's ex-boss had been a man whose first name she now knew, thanks to that hidden email folder. If her program at home was working well and running as it should, she'd soon know his last name. That meant she would be able to find out if he was still here.

And using the FBI wifi, it might just be possible to hack into his machine - hopefully undetectably. Then at least, she'd know if he was one of the good guys - or one of the others.

The thought was very scary, and she didn't want to dwell on it because if she did, she was sure that Connor would sense something was wrong with that unerringly accurate instinct she had. So as soon as she had finished her burger and drunk half her soda, she checked the phone again, keeping her mind firmly on work.

And there it was. She'd gotten into this water-damaged phone.

"Right. I've accessed it," she said proudly.

"Can you get into the messages?" Connor had finished his own burger and was wiping his fingers, checking his emails, and taking a look at other case files as he sat on the opposite side of his desk.

"Yes and no," Cami said. "I'm only getting some of them. This phone isn't just water damage. It also had an impact on the water surface, and that has blitzed a portion of its hard drive."

She frowned as she read what she had. These were from a different number that she could tell, although she still couldn't see all of them. This man who had stolen the phones must have built up a store of them and was now using them as his weapons, she realized.

"These texts," she said, surprised. "I've got a piece of one of them here. Not the whole thing, but it's making it sound as if he was right there. Right with these women."

"How do you mean?" Connor sounded confused.

"He's saying where they are. Listen to this. 'I can see you turning the corner now. You have a great view of the park from there, don't you?' And listen to this one. 'I know where you are walking, short-haired sweetheart. You're going out onto the bridge.'"

She shook her head. "I can't see more. I'm sure there is more, though."

Connor's eyebrows raised.

"So he's basically using those texts to make these women believe he's tracking them closely."

"Yes," Cami said. "Clearly, that's making them scared. Scared enough of being followed and what he might do to them to do things that then end up being dangerous. And in these two cases, they ended up being deadly."

She felt shivers cascading down her spine as she thought about the evil of that action. It was the most terrible thing she could think of to fool someone into believing they were being followed and pursued. And now she could see why these two women were the victims. Because both of them seemed to have shared a similar mindset. They were fearful people who were wary of strangers and who would often believe what they were told, even if it wasn't necessarily true. That was exactly what they'd been told about Pippa and Vicky.

"I think he's picking people who he thinks will scare easily," she said.

"But how is he tracking them?" Connor said.

Cami shook her head reluctantly. That was, unfortunately, where she was stumped.

"I can't tell," she admitted.

"He couldn't have installed tracking software on the phones?"

Cami shook her head. "It doesn't look like it on the other phone, the one that was crushed. And there's definitely nothing on this phone. I can tell because I can access a portion of the main menu, and I see enough to make out that it has an actual app that prevents location tracking. It's a good and reliable app, and I know it works."

No wonder Vicky had been so scared. She'd had an app in place, and still, someone had been targeting her.

"Any way of getting around it?"

Cami thought hard.

"I guess the only people who might be able to know a specific phone's location would be the workers at the data center itself. And I can look that up, see where it is."

Now that she thought about it, it was surely possible that someone at the data center might have bypassed that app, tracked the phone's location, and targeted the women that way, enjoying the thrill and the sense of fear as he watched them run, watched them flee, and get into dangerous or deadly situations.

Connor nodded in agreement. "That's a good idea. We should follow up on that lead and see what we can find out."

Cami turned to her new job, locating the data center where this phone was registered and the hub that it was operated from.

"We're in luck," she said. "This center is in Boston. It's north of downtown. I guess it's half an hour away?" She paused. "The problem is that it's closed now. Skeleton staff only after hours, it says here, and he's been doing this tracking during the day, and the early evenings, from the timing of the messages. That means he would have been accessing the phones at work, in business hours."

Connor nodded. "Okay. That's tomorrow's job, then. First thing tomorrow. We meet here at seven-thirty? That's good with you?"

"Yes. That's good with me," Cami said.

"You want a ride home?" Connor asked, but Cami shook her head. Kieran's apartment was further away from the FBI offices than the MIT student accommodation had been, and Connor also needed to get home to his life - and his fiancée and his cats.

"I'll catch a cab," she said. "See you in the morning."

"Thank you. See you then," he replied.

As she walked downstairs, the thought came to her again.

Liam's boss. His surname might soon be known to her. And when she knew it, she could start finding out more.

Maybe even tomorrow.

It would all depend on what was uncovered when she got back to Kieran's place tonight.

CHAPTER SIXTEEN

"You're home?"

Cami could hear the note of surprised happiness in Kieran's voice as he heard her key in the lock. By the time she opened it, he was there, dressed in his jeans and T-shirt that hugged his broad shoulders, a smile on his face.

"It's a very local case," she explained. "We didn't have to travel anywhere, and there wasn't anything else we could do tonight."

"I'm glad to see you, but I wish I'd known. I would have organized extra food. I made one portion of stir fry and ate all of it."

"I had a burger at work. My boss bought it for me," Cami explained. She felt glad and relieved to be walking into the warm apartment, to be hanging her jacket up on the coat stand. This felt like coming home, and she had to remind herself that Kieran's kind offer didn't come with an indefinite time limit. It wasn't like she'd signed a year's lease. He might want her out at any time, and even if he didn't say so, she needed to be considerate and not overstay her welcome. After all, it was a one-bedroom place, and you couldn't exactly have friends come around when your housemate was sleeping on the couch with all her clothes on the bookshelf. No, she was going to need to move on.

But not right now. Now, it was amazing to come home to this. It was like the family atmosphere she'd never had. Or if she had, it was too long ago for her to remember, way back before things with her father had soured, and then Jenna had vanished.

"I'm glad you've at least had some food. I've just boiled the kettle to make hot chocolate. Want some?"

"I'd love some."

It felt good that Kieran was so amped to see her. It made her feel happy. And she felt exactly the same way.

"So," she said. "Let's see what these hidden files are showing."

The seriousness of their predicament was now intruding on the satisfaction of homecoming. Both she and Kieran were in danger, and they couldn't forget it.

While Kieran brought through two steaming cups of hot chocolate, Cami powered up the laptop she'd left to run. And it had run, she saw. It had managed to retrieve what was there. The problem was that it wasn't very much.

Cami felt disappointment surge through her. She had hoped that the hidden files would reveal more. But things had been deleted and overwritten, and now there wasn't very much to be found.

However, her gaze sharpened as she saw more of that email that Liam had written to his boss was now visible. Enough to see the recipient's ID. And now, she had a full name. His boss's name was Bill Oertel. That was an unusual name. Not too common.

Sipping her hot chocolate, Cami looked it up. She had no idea if Bill Oertel was good or bad or if he was still with the FBI or not. But she could at least get a picture of who he was.

Here he was. She'd found his profile online.

He was still with the FBI. This is his current work profile here. He looked about Connor's age. He had light brown hair and a smooth expression, and she couldn't tell the color of his eyes from that small photo.

He'd been with the FBI for nine years. That meant he would have been there when Jenna went missing. He would most likely have had time to be promoted before and since then. Was he the one who was involved in this? Or was he an innocent person whose career and life might also be at risk?

She wished she knew. His face gave nothing away. If only she could tell, from the photo, what was really going on in his mind.

She looked up to see Kieran staring at her, looking concerned.

"Has it picked up anything, Cami?"

She nodded. "I have the full name of Liam's boss at the time. He was the one who, I think, told Liam to drop the case, but I don't know if it was his idea. I don't know if he's a good or bad guy. Did Ethan ever mention someone called Bill Oertel?"

"Bill Oertel?" Kieran repeated the words, and she could see he was thinking very carefully about this. He knew how important it was, and he was racking his brains for any mention of the words.

"No, sorry, Cami, I don't remember. But that doesn't mean anything because I don't think Ethan was telling me everything. I think he was being careful not to say stuff," Kieran said apologetically.

Cami nodded, understanding. She took another sip of her hot chocolate, feeling the warmth spread through her body. She needed to think needed to come up with a plan.

"What do we do now?" Kieran asked, breaking the silence.

Cami looked at him. "We need to find out more about Bill Oertel. See if we can uncover anything about him. Ideally, we somehow need to hack his devices."

"You think you can do that?"

Cami shrugged. "I don't know. Let me see what I can find on him."

She went looking online. Bill Oertel was single, although he seemed to have had a few girlfriends in the past, and she thought there might have been a divorce way back. He loved extreme sports. He was a parachutist and a hang glider. That was all in the public domain because he was a member of the sports clubs. But she couldn't see much about his private life. That side, he seemed to keep well hidden.

"I am going to try to send him an email, just to see if I can get a backdoor into his devices," Cami decided.

She had a few fake email addresses in her arsenal. Like every hacker did. Hers were carefully hidden and designed so that they didn't trace back to her at all.

She composed an email based on an extreme sports event that she saw he'd attended recently. It contained a link to a feedback form that competitors were asked to fill in. Cami even created a fake form that he could go ahead and complete just to make the page seem real. Just in case. But if he clicked on it, then he'd be giving her a backdoor into his devices. Her software would instantly latch onto it, and then the path would be open.

He might take the bait. She thought the email looked authentic and the story was plausible.

"I've done what I can," she said. "We'll have to wait now and see what the morning brings."

Would he click on it? She couldn't let herself think about it, or she'd get too anxious. That was another attribute Connor had taught her, to focus on what you could work on and to be calm about what you couldn't.

Now, it was time to use the miniature bathroom, with the amazingly hot and powerful shower, and get ready for bed. She needed her sleep.

Without looking too closely at Kieran, Cami hurried to the shower. She showered quickly, enjoying the warmth, using some of the fancy shower gel she'd bought as her contribution toward the running of the

71

household – together with the ciders, a funny doormat, a new set of drinking glasses, and a week's worth of groceries.

She was eager to see what the morning brought in terms of the case. The case was what she needed to focus on now.

Not Bill Oertel. And not Kieran. Not now.

While this killer-by-text was out there and at large, Cami needed to focus on finding him. Because she had a nasty feeling that if he was sleeping at all, he'd be up early and on the hunt.

CHAPTER SEVENTEEN

The data center was a bustling hive of activity when Cami and Connor arrived there just before eight a.m. She felt hopeful that this would provide a breakthrough in the case and finally allow them to catch the predator who was stalking these women.

"How can I help you?" The young, blond receptionist in the lobby looked harassed and was typing furiously on her keyboard, frowning from behind her blue-rimmed eyeglasses. Cami got the impression she was there more to fend off the public while doing her own work than she was to welcome them in. After all, the data center was like a big back office where administrative work was done. Not a front office place where sales were made.

"FBI," Connor said, showing his badge. That got her attention. Her fingers froze. She looked up, taking them both in for the first time.

"FBI?" she echoed. "Why are you here?"

"We are investigating two suspicious deaths," Connor said. "The data center used by both the victims' phones is this one. We need to take a look at your systems and to see if anyone here was able to access these phones' locations."

"I'm going to call my manager," the receptionist said immediately, getting on the phone.

They didn't have to wait long. Just a minute later, a harassed-looking man with a phone in his hand and a clipboard under his arm appeared through a side door.

"Richard, these are FBI officers," the receptionist said. "And they want to know something about our systems."

His brown eyes widened. "Our systems. What do you want to know?"

Cami waited while Connor patiently repeated his request.

"You think someone in our data center is doing this?" The man sounded horrified by the thought. "I'm sure that's impossible."

"We need to check it out," Connor insisted.

With an effort, the flustered manager pulled himself together.

"Come to my office, please," he said, leading them away from the receptionist's curious stare.

Cami followed him and Connor along the corridor, into an elevator, and up to the building's third floor. His office was spacious, with a view of the city center nearby. There were several computer monitors on the wall. A stream of data was being filtered down on the screens.

"We're doing updates," he explained. "So this is a difficult time."

Connor nodded. "I don't think there would ever be an easy time in a place as large and busy as this," he acknowledged. "However, we need to see all the activity logs from the past few days, so we can figure out who had access to what. And we'll also need real-time access to your servers."

Richard hesitated. "I don't know if I can do that. I mean, our clients trust us with their data. We can't just hand this over to anyone."

"We're not going to use the data or even take it off-site," Connor reassured him. "All we need is to see it, so we can work out whether anyone in this building might have been tracking cellphones. You'd surely also want to know if any of your staff were doing that?"

"Absolutely, absolutely," he agreed. "But I don't see how it's possible, though. Because all our computers are very strictly locked, outside of when they are actually active. We have good security systems in place. I'll show you."

He moved to the keyboard and tapped a few keys. The feed on the closest monitor changed. Now Cami looked closely as she saw the data populate the screen.

"Here you go. You can see all our active connections here at a glance. The location of the phones themselves isn't even visible. You'd need to go into an individual record to access it, and for that, you'd need a password and to connect up to one of the master servers."

Cami looked closely at the feed. The manager was scrolling it back, taking the activity history back a few hours to last night and then to yesterday evening. There were several different computers that were being used, she saw, her mind accelerating as she figured out the logic that was in use here and how the systems ran.

"Wait," she said.

The manager turned to her, surprised. "Sorry, ma'am, what?"

"I've seen something," she said. As the data had scrolled by, she'd spotted an anomaly. Something on one of the machines didn't match up with the data stream on the others.

"Just pause it," she said. Then she walked up to the screen and physically pointed to the row of data.

"I don't know your systems well, but to me, it looks as if this computer has been operating full-time with its password in place. Look. All the others go into dark mode, and the data stops running when people log off; you can see it. But not that one. It's like someone put in a master password, and it's never been deactivated."

The manager stared at her, looking surprised. Then he stared back at the screen.

"That computer? I didn't even notice it. It passed me right by."

"I'm correct, aren't I?"

"I - I guess you're correct about that, but I still don't see how it's possible. That's our computer which is used for staff training. It's not normally used for everyday activities. It's in the back office that's only opened up for training sessions." He stared at the screen again, shaking his head. "You're right, though. You're right. Let's go and see what's happening there."

The manager, now looking even more stressed than he had done, led the way along the corridor, down a floor, and then into a big room with sets of tables lined up inside.

"You see, this is the room we use for training, and the master computer is beyond."

He walked inside. He tapped a key to activate the screen. And the activity log popped up on it, live and ready to go.

"This is very unusual," he murmured. "Well, I'll log out immediately and get this password changed."

"No, wait!" Cami said. "Wait. Before you do that, I want to know - can anyone in the company log into this machine remotely? From their own work desk?"

He stared at her, frowning.

Then he nodded. "Yes," he said. "This computer might be connected to online users elsewhere in the building."

"Then don't disconnect it," she said. "Because we need to see who's linked up to it right now. Nobody should be? And then, we look at the data logs from yesterday if nobody is."

"Of course. Of course, we can do that."

He moved forward and began pressing keys quickly.

Cami personally thought he should have volunteered this information. She had no idea whether he was just too shocked to have thought of it, too intimidated by the law enforcement presence, or else trying to protect himself for not having picked up that the computer access hadn't been deactivated. But either way, she had seen immediately that this computer could act as a hub where other online users could log in.

Nobody was monitoring this particular machine, tucked away behind the training room. So someone had been having carte blanche with it, and now it was time to find out whom. She was keeping a close eye on the manager, just in case protecting his employees ended up being more important to him than helping the police.

But he seemed to be logging into the user record and not trying to cover any tracks.

"Okay," the manager said, finally straightening up and turning to them. "Here's the detail. The employee who is logged on at this moment is Johnny Chalmers."

"Has Johnny Chalmers been going into the cellphone user records?"

The manager nodded. "There's activity in those records, yes. I see he's accessing one now. I can pull the logs to see which other ones have been accessed, but it looks like quite a few yesterday. Forty or fifty." His eyebrows raised. "It'll take time to click on each one and see who they are, but I can do it if you need me to."

"Who's Mr. Chalmers?" Connor asked. "Is he in the building now? He should be, correct if he's accessing this?"

Cami agreed. Right now, getting to Johnny Chalmers was more important than accessing the records to see where he'd been.

"He is in the building," the manager said. "He works on this floor, in the second admin office."

"And through this machine, this open connection, he would have been able to track the locations of various cellphones that fall under this data center?"

The manager was now wringing his hands miserably.

"Yes, yes, he would. As I said, I don't know how we didn't pick up on it before now. He can't have been doing it for long. This computer was reset two weeks ago."

Two weeks was all it would have taken. He might even have found a way to illegally harness his own cellphone into the tracking network. The manager had said that wasn't possible, but then again, he'd also said that there were no open computers. The manager was underplaying this likelihood and protecting himself.

Chalmers might have logged in here to get the records and then continued to track some of them outside of work, at a coffee shop, or a public place where he could see the victims' reactions.

"Let's go and speak to him straight away," Connor said.

The manager led the way, now hustling through the corridors and bursting into an open-plan office where four employees were bent over their keyboards, checking data from long lists.

"Er, Johnny," the manager said in apologetic tones. "The FBI is here. They want to -"

He never finished his sentence.

Johnny Chalmers looked up as soon as they walked in. He was at the desk furthest away from the door, in the corner of the room. He was a tall man with brown hair straggling over his shirt collar and wide, pale blue eyes. Horror filled them as he saw the FBI walk in.

The next moment, he jumped up from his desk, turned, and bolted for the fire door at the back of the room.

Wrenching it open, he raced out, fleeing down the fire stairs, his frantic footsteps clanging on the steel.

CHAPTER EIGHTEEN

"Stop!" Cami heard Connor's voice ring out. And the next moment, her boss had taken off in pursuit, rushing across the office floor, heading for that same fire door. He flung it all the way open and set off, his footsteps even louder and faster than Johnny Chalmers' had been.

Cami hurried over to the window, looking out to see if she could spot the fleeing duo as pandemonium filled the office. The manager was trying to restore calm, shouting to the employees who had abandoned their desks and were now also crowding to the window to see the chase.

And it was a chase, Cami saw. Johnny was using his long legs and his lean, strong build to its full advantage. He was powering across the building's courtyard, heading for a side exit point.

No way she could catch up. But she needed to do something while Connor tried his best to close the gap. She needed to use her initiative here because Johnny knew the layout of this office complex and Connor didn't, and what if he lost this suspect? What if he ran right out of the premises?

That got Cami thinking.

That was the only way he could successfully flee. If he left the premises. So how could she ensure that he didn't?

She turned to the manager.

"The main gate!" she said. "It needs to be closed. Is there a security guard, someone in charge, there?"

He nodded, looking wide-eyed and breathless.

"Yes, there is," he agreed.

"Get on the phone to him, now. Tell him nobody must leave. Not in a car, not on foot. He must close the gate and stop them."

The manager nodded and raised his cell phone, stabbing hurriedly at the numbers.

That took care of the front entrance. But a big place like this might have another exit point, Cami realized. How could she locate it?

Her thoughts went immediately to IT, to screens, but then she realized she was thinking wrong. On the wall was a simple old-fashioned layout map near the fire door, with the building's exit points marked, which would give her what she needed.

Rushing over, she took a look.

Yes, she was right. There was another exit point on the south side of the building. It looked like it might be used for deliveries. And she thought that Johnny might just end up running there, especially if he saw that the front entrance was being blocked.

Would she be on time? She guessed it would all depend on what Johnny did. If he'd gone straight for the service entrance, she might not be in time.

As Cami pounded out of the room, retracing her steps to the main lobby, she found herself going through the logic in her own mind, her thoughts keeping pace with her frantic strides.

If he'd gone straight to the service entrance, then Connor would have seen him. But if he'd managed to get out of sight, if he'd lost Connor for a while, then he might have gotten a lead.

She needed to get there, and fast!

"Sorry, sorry!" Cami twisted sideways as she sped through the lobby, narrowly avoiding a man walking in, carrying a briefcase in one hand and a cup of coffee in the other. She hurried to the glass doors, pushed them open, and burst out.

Now, here she was, with the map layout still in her mind, but needing a moment to orient herself now that she was all the way out here. Where could it be?

To the left. There would be a shortcut leading to the left. That was what the map had told her.

Cami sprinted to the left, her heart pounding in her chest. She could hear the sound of footsteps in the distance, beyond another row of office buildings, but she didn't know whether they belonged to Johnny or Connor or to someone else entirely. They could even be coming from outside the office complex. By now, Connor could have caught this fugitive. She hoped so.

But she had to get to that service entrance, just in case.

What was the quickest way? Down here? She sprinted past a loading dock and a series of parked trucks. One of them was pulling into its bay. She wasn't going to stop. It could stop. Cami didn't even slow down as she ran along, hearing the annoyed blare of the driver's horn but not caring because what was important now was to catch this fleeing man.

There was the entrance. Hemmed in by tall wire fencing, the gate was closed. That gave her a moment of relief. But then, anxiety flared again as her angle changed, and she saw it better. It wasn't closed. It was partially open. Not enough for a car, but more than enough for a person to get out of it.

And as she had that thought, she realized that her guess had been right. The footsteps were getting louder, and they were definitely coming from the other side of the office building. They were fast and frantic and heading her way.

Johnny was fleeing in this direction. And she had to try to stop him.

If she could get there first, she might be able to get that gate closed, and then he'd be able to fight the gate rather than fighting her. Cami didn't want him to fight her. She knew she'd lose. He was nearly a foot taller than her with long arms and probably weighed sixty pounds more than she did.

And she was finding it difficult to get up the speed she needed to in order to get a lead on him. If she didn't get a lead, then her decisions would be severely limited. She might lose him.

Her legs were burning. Her Doc Martens were thudding over the paving. She misstepped and stumbled, her heart rate now peaking with stress, but caught herself before she actually face-planted at speed on that hard concrete walkway.

There he was!

Desperation written all over his face, Johnny Chalmers had rounded the corner and was now hurtling toward the same point she was.

She was ahead. But she was going to be mowed down by this man. He was hell-bent on getting out of that gate. How could she stop him without being physically attacked herself?

Cami glanced at him again, her stomach twisting as she saw he'd seen her and was now running even faster. She didn't know where Connor was. Had he lost Johnny completely?

As she got closer, she saw that there was a chain which was looped over one side of the gate. And there was a padlock on it. But the padlock was closed on the open chain. Presumably, they'd open it and then relock it when the gate was fastened up at night.

So she had a gate, ajar just a crack. She had a chain. And she had a closed padlock. Those were all she had against a man running as if his life depended on it.

How could she use them?

How could she make a plan to stop this man who was now channeling all the qualities of a runaway train?

Suddenly, the answer came to Cami.

She saw she was going to get there first. She'd have about a three-second lead on him before he arrived and used his speed to burst through that gate while mowing her down.

Cami reached the gate. Grabbed it with her right hand. She pulled it open, and charged through it. Then she spun around, closed it, and dragged the chain through the gap so that it was holding the gate closed.

She was holding the chain firmly. And she was now on the other side of the gate. The chain itself was keeping the gate closed.

But would it be enough? Cami braced herself, clinging to the chain with all her strength as Johnny arrived, legs pounding frantically, and crashed against the gate with his full body weight.

CHAPTER NINETEEN

Cami tugged the ends of the chain together with all her force, hanging on for dear life as the gate rocked and swayed.

"Let go!" Johnny yelled, the sound waves battering her as he tried his best to rattle and twist that chain right out of her hands.

"No!" she yelled back, clutching it even harder.

She was glad she was on the other side of the gate, but he was now wrenching violently at the chain, doing everything he could to get it free. Bearing all her weight against it, Cami hung on, knowing she couldn't do so forever and that if he got lucky, he might burst right out of this service entrance.

If he did, then she was sure he'd vanish. Beyond the gate was an underpass leading into a warren of urban streets. If he got through, he could scuttle along that underpass and melt into the network of alleyways.

A jerk from him nearly tugged her right off her feet. She could feel the chain slipping out of her grasp; she could feel herself losing her grip.

And then, with a thud of feet, Connor rounded the corner, racing toward them.

"Hands in the air," he yelled. "You are under arrest, Johnny Chalmers. Hands in the air!"

Johnny let go of the chain, to Cami's extreme relief. Her fingers were burning from the effort, and the chain had pinched the palm of her hand so hard she thought she might get a blood blister. It was throbbing. But at least she'd managed to stop him from escaping.

And now they could ask him the tough questions. Like: why had he been accessing and tracking people's phones?

Now, Cami saw the fight had gone out of their fleeing suspect. His adrenaline had ebbed, and she thought he would have been too exhausted to try and run again, even if Connor hadn't produced a pair of handcuffs. But her boss and partner weren't taking any chances. He handcuffed Johnny and then quickly searched him. The search produced a cell phone in his jacket pocket, which Cami was very glad to see. She was sure that he'd been using this phone to send messages.

She could see it from the appalled expression on his face as Connor took it from him and placed it carefully into a plastic bag.

Then, they marched him back the way they had come.

Cami followed, seeing interested faces crowding the office windows as they returned to the car.

"Get in and I don't want any trouble," Connor said firmly, attaching the handcuffs to the steel bracket in the back seat.

Cami knew how that felt. She couldn't help a pang as she recalled exactly what it had been like when she'd been arrested by the FBI after hacking their site. She could see from the crestfallen expression on Johnny's face that he was now taking in the full reality of his predicament.

"You did a good job there, Cami," Connor finally had the chance to say after closing the back door on their suspect, who was still breathing rapidly and was now looking down at his cuffed, firmly fastened hands in consternation.

"I figured out there was a service entrance from the diagram on the wall and thought it might help to go there," she said, feeling pleased.

"And it did. He managed to dodge into a back room and got out of a side door which he then blockaded behind him. So I had to backtrack," Connor explained.

"He's clearly done everything he can to escape," Cami said, feeling astounded by the lengths he'd gone to.

"Time to find out why," Connor said grimly. "We might as well take him straight back to the FBI offices and question him there. We're so close by in any case."

Cami climbed into the front. She could still feel her heart was in overdrive from the stress and action of the pursuit. It really wasn't what she was made for. She was shaking all over after having faced that chain-rattling, frantic man down at the gate. And yet, she'd managed it and felt a sense of exhausted pride that she'd been able to help.

But now, they'd need to link up his activities to the crimes. Cami knew from experience that this might not be easy. Some criminals and killers resisted every step of the way. She wondered if Johnny Chalmers would be one of them.

*

Twenty minutes later, Johnny was sitting in the interview room at the FBI offices. His face was still flushed, although his breathing had calmed down. His gaze was darting everywhere. Pinned in the steel chair behind the table, he looked thoroughly trapped.

And, when Cami and Connor walked in, he didn't even wait before starting to talk.

"I didn't do anything wrong," Johnny protested, his voice shaking. "I swear. I don't even know what I'm doing here. This is all so unfair. Why did you even arrest me?"

Cami exchanged a glance with Connor. They'd heard this before. This was nothing new. Pleading innocence, Cami knew, would get Johnny precisely nowhere.

"You were tracking people's phones," Connor said. "That's why you're here, Mr. Chalmers. You were linked up to an open computer in the training room that had the master password activated. And now, we're going to take a look at your phone and find out exactly what you were doing with that information."

Johnny turned sheet white. "Wait! You - you can't do that! My phone's my private property!"

"Not if it's been used for illegal activities. And we have unfortunately found out you've been abusing your position at work to track people's phones.

"I didn't mean to hurt anyone," Johnny blurted out, his voice shaking. "I just wanted to feel connected to someone, you know? And tracking their phones, it made me feel like I was a part of their lives. But I swear I didn't have any bad intentions."

"You have a choice," Connor told him inexorably. "Open this phone now for us, or we'll open it. And if we open it, there are going to be additional items on what is already a very long charge sheet."

"It's my private property," Johnny grumbled.

"Okay," Connor said. "We're going to take you down to the holding cells while Cami opens the phone."

"What?" Now he sat bolt upright, sounding aghast.

"Your choice," Connor said in tones that Cami knew were carefully designed to sound harassed and uncaring.

"It probably won't take me that long," Cami reassured him. "Most times, I can get it open in a few hours. A day at the most." She felt cruel when she saw his dismayed expression, but really, all he had to do was to cooperate. He was just making things harder for everyone right now.

"A day?"

"You're the one who's not willing to open it. If it takes two days, that's how long you sit inside," Connor said.

"Okay, okay." Faced with this threat, their suspect had broken. "I'll open it. But I want you to know that this meant nothing. It was just some innocent fun on my side."

"I'm sure it was. On your side," Connor echoed as Cami went and got the phone out of the bag. It took a quick code input from Johnny, and it was open. She could have cracked that in a few minutes, she thought.

"Now, show us what you've been doing."

He handled the phone with some difficulty in his handcuffs, and Cami walked around to check that he wasn't erasing anything along the way. But now, she thought, he'd finally realized the game was up. He scrolled straight through to a series of messages.

"Hey, beautiful! Do you live on Princes Street, or are you just walking that way?"

"Listen, cutie, when you pass Big Bite Burgers, how about going in and waiting for me? I can come to meet you there."

Cami read the messages out to Connor. They had been sent to a few different phone numbers. Just one or two texts per number. He'd been doing it for a little longer than a week. Clearly, he'd focused on female cellphone users, and he must have picked those out after accessing the records.

But what she wasn't seeing was texts to either of the numbers belonging to the victims. Not yesterday, not the day before, not two days before that.

And clearly, Johnny had been using his personal cellphone to message his targets, not a burner phone. There were distinct differences in the MO that she was picking up here.

"It was just a bit of fun," he said in a quivering voice, now horrified at being faced with the implications of his actions.

"I'm sure it was," Connor said.

"The texts that he's sent are from this phone, his personal device," Cami said. "They're all on here."

"No other phones on you, clearly. Did you purchase or steal any spare phones in the past few days?"

Johnny shook his head vigorously. "I'm not a thief! Why would I buy a spare phone?"

Cami saw a blank lack of understanding in his gaze, and she believed him.

Connor raised his eyebrows. "In that case, you'd better tell us where you were yesterday, in the late afternoon, from about four p.m. onward. Go on, Mr. Chalmers. Tell us your whereabouts. If you're cleared, then we'll leave this from our side. If you can't provide a confirmable alibi, then I'll need to search your work desk, your car, and your home for any evidence of additional phones."

"Yesterday, I was in a meeting at work. We were all sitting in the conference room," he said. "It lasted from three p.m. until five-thirty p.m. During that time, I had to give a presentation. My presentation was from four-thirty to five p.m. I mean, I was standing in front of the group and going through some slides on our stats at that time."

Connor nodded slowly, and Cami knew that timeframe cleared him. "Okay. You're lucky. The fact you were in that meeting, giving a presentation, clears you of a potentially more serious crime. But we're still going to hand you over to the local police and inform your company of what you've done."

Now, Johnny's eyes were filling with tears. "I'm so sorry. So sorry."

Connor nodded. "The fact you ran from us shows me that you were feeling guilt," he said in a surprisingly kindly tone. "You're going to suffer the consequences, but they won't be as bad as they could have been. You might get away with a first-offense warning or a suspended sentence if they're feeling in a compassionate mood. But I want you to think carefully about what you did. What it could have led to. We all have choices. If you choose badly, it can take you down a very dark road. Be glad you've had this chance to be called back from it."

He looked like he was going to say more, but at that point his phone rang.

He glanced at Cami and stood up immediately. She did too. His body language clued her that this might be an important call.

Connor took it before he'd even left the room, and his expression as he listened to the voice on the other end told her something bad had happened.

Something really bad.

CHAPTER TWENTY

"It's happened again."

Cami stared at Connor in horror as he spoke the words.

"It's happened again - at any rate, they suspect so. Just fifteen minutes ago, near the city center, a young woman ran into oncoming traffic. Witnesses say she was staring at her phone and seemed frantically upset. She didn't seem to realize what she was doing or that the light was against her."

Cami felt her stomach clench.

They'd tried so hard to find him, but Johnny Chalmers was not their suspect, and now, this invisible man had done it again.

"We're going to go to the scene now," Connor said. "Go down to the car and wait there while I brief someone in the office on how to handle Mr. Chalmers."

He strode away, and Cami rushed down to the car with her heart thudding hard. This was so terrible. She felt frantic with the need to prevent this from happening because it felt unstoppable. As if this man was picking out people and using his evil powers over them to drive them out of their minds with stress and worry, with lethal consequences.

She twined her fingers together, clasping them tightly, hoping that this new scene might give them a lead or give them something, at least.

Having done his briefing, Connor rushed down and climbed in on the driver's side. Then, they sped away, heading for the crossroads where this latest crime had happened.

Cami realized it wasn't going to be a long drive. Like the others, this location was close by. Not far at all from the FBI offices and once again clearly in this killer's 'hood.

She saw the scene up ahead, the red and white flashing lights cutting the drizzle. Traffic had been rerouted, and Connor had to stop on the road and show his ID to one of the cops before being waved through. Then, they sped along the now-empty road to the scene up ahead.

Cami swallowed as she saw it. The ambulance lights flashed. Police cars are parked on either side.

And the body.

Except - it wasn't a body. Her heart skipped a beat as she realized that this woman was still alive. She was obviously very seriously hurt. But the paramedics were bent over her, and as Connor watched, they eased her onto a stretcher.

"Morning. Agent Connor and Cami Lark," Connor introduced them briefly. "What's the situation with this victim?"

The policeman who was managing the scene turned to face him. "Her name's Mindy Knowles, her home address is just a few blocks away; her age is twenty-three. She has a bad concussion, a broken leg, and a few broken ribs, it looks like. They're going to rush her to the ICU."

"Where's her phone?" Connor asked. "I believe she was holding a phone? We need to access that phone because there are messages on it that we need to read."

"The phone is here," the officer said. "We've got it, as well as her purse. You're welcome to take it. I should warn you, though, that the screen was smashed in the impact, and it won't be usable."

"That's okay. We just need to get some information off it, and then we can give it back to you to keep with her other possessions," Connor said.

"Ready? Got her. Okay."

With practiced ease, the paramedics carefully transferred the prone woman to the stretcher. Cami stared in dismay. Her face was grazed, she was bleeding from a nasty gash in her head, her auburn hair was tangled, and she'd been totally knocked out. Probably a good thing because her other injuries must be agonizing, Cami thought. She was so limp that her coat was just about slipping off her. In fact, as Cami watched, something fell out of the pocket and landed on the road.

"You want to get that?" the paramedic asked his partner.

"Wait!" Cami rushed forward, wanting a better look at that familiar object. "I just need to see what that is?"

Suddenly, a new idea was occurring to her about how the killer might have done this and how he'd managed to work in the way he had. How he'd tracked them.

"Look at this," she said to Connor. This white object, just a little larger than a button, might provide the clues they needed.

"What is it?" he asked.

"It's an air tag. It's a device that can be used for remote tracking. Connor, I think we're learning how he's been doing this. It was in her coat pocket?" she asked.

"Yes, ma'am," the paramedic replied. "It was in there, and it slipped out just as we lifted her."

Cami nodded.

"We need to look again at the other victims. To see if they also had air tags on their persons. I think this is how he's doing it; I really do. Now it makes sense."

Connor stepped forward and carefully transferred the air tag to an evidence bag. Then Cami stepped back, allowing the paramedics to transfer the stretcher to the ambulance. In a moment, with a wail of sirens, they were gone.

"The contents of Vicky's purse are scattered in the river," Connor said thoughtfully. "The purse was found, but it was totally empty. Her jacket was brought in with her and thoroughly searched. I don't recall seeing an air tag being listed, and it could well have been washed away. But Pippa might have had one on her, and if she did, then we can search for it."

Connor quickly scrolled through his phone, checking for information on where Pippa's possessions would be now.

"Okay. They were taken from the autopsy room to the local police station for safekeeping, and they're in the evidence room."

He turned away, walking purposefully to his car, and Cami followed. Her mind was whirling. Air tags. So that was how he'd tracked them? He must have been very sneaky to have somehow planted them on these careful, fearful and paranoid women. How had he done that?

They climbed into the car and headed for the police station, which was only a couple of blocks away. Arriving there, Connor parked and hurried in, with Cami following close behind.

"We're here to see the belongings of Pippa Ross," Connor said. "They would probably have been brought here yesterday afternoon." He showed his badge. "And we need a desk to work at, also."

The officer looked at a computer and then consulted a paper list.

"Yes. Those belongings have been taken into evidence. If you come through, we can release them for you to have a look."

The young officer at the front desk escorted Cami and Connor through to the back office, and they sat and waited while he went to the evidence room to fetch them.

While they waited, Cami took the smashed phone and linked it up to her own phone and laptop. Even though the screen was smashed, if she could bypass the security on it, then she'd be able to see the messages via her own phone.

Just as she'd gotten her access program running, the officer came back with a large cardboard box.

"Here you go," he said. "In here is her purse, her jacket, and a few other items of clothing, as well as her shoes."

Cami checked the list of evidence. It didn't mention an air tag, but she was going to stay hopeful. After all, it might have just been very well hidden.

"I'm going to search her jacket," Connor said. "Do you want to search the purse?"

Those were the two most likely hiding places where someone could have hidden a tag. Cami applied herself to the search, working as thoroughly as she could. The purse had one main compartment and one side zipper compartment. She searched them both carefully, looking at everything, feeling around with her fingers to make sure she didn't miss anything.

Oh, and here was something else she hadn't even seen the first time. It was a small, hidden compartment that Cami was sure was useful for cash or cards to be stashed away.

What was in here? It looked like nothing. But to make sure, she stuck her fingers in.

And they came out holding an air tag that was identical to the one they'd found on the latest victim.

She showed it to Connor and saw his eyes widen.

"This is how he's doing it," she said. "He's putting them into their jackets or their purses, and then he's messaging them. He's making them do what they do. But who is he?"

She stared at Connor, seeing him nod slowly, knowing that this man's identity was crucial - and yet, how could they find out more about him?

Then, Cami's phone beeped again and signaled that she had access to Mindy's iPhone. Full access to a phone that was undamaged apart from its shattered screen.

"This is the first time we're going to be able to read all the messages he sent," she said to Connor. "And this could be our game changer."

CHAPTER TWENTY ONE

The fingersmith wanted to leap and jump and dance with delight as he hurried back into the mall. What a success that had been. He'd actually managed to get a glimpse of her because she'd been so close by. The woman had been looking absolutely haunted by the time she'd misjudged the light and, in a total panic, simply rushed into oncoming traffic.

The shrill scream of brakes had been music to his ears. He guessed she might have survived, but she'd be badly hurt. He hoped she died, though, because if she did, it was his ultimate achievement realized.

He was the magical one, the person who had powers over life and death, whose abilities transcended the normal in almost every way.

He sat down at the coffee kiosk and quickly read through the messages he'd sent. These had worked really well, perfectly, in fact, and he needed to make a note of how he had done this and what he had said. Because he'd gotten it so right this time. So right. It had been perfection.

It was all working out just as he'd planned. His victims were falling into his trap, and he was loving every moment of it. The satisfaction of watching them do exactly what he made them do as if they were under his full control, was indescribable.

Most definitely, it seemed to work well when he said he was inside their mind. And he knew exactly what terminology to use. That was easy, given his background. He guessed he was so familiar with it that the words rolled out of him.

The way he'd said that, he was inside her head, watching her. That this was a powerful magic based on the influence of dark forces from beyond the grave. That he'd always be there now, with her. That he had used his powers to infiltrate her brain. That she didn't know it, but he'd hypnotized her earlier on, and now she couldn't get away from him.

It had been so easy to make her believe him, to make her accept that he was some sort of dark and powerful force that was controlling her every move. And she had fallen for it, hook, line, and sinker.

He scrolled through the messages again, feeling a sense of pride in his work. He had been able to manipulate her so easily, and the results had been exactly what he had wanted.

She hadn't been able to think or reason. His messages, the content as well as the timing of them, had filled her mind, and that made him feel deeply contented. It was amazing how effective it was. So many threatening texts in such quick succession had the most incredible impact on them.

He had a powerful talent. Now that he was tapping his own ability, he could see how strong it was. It wasn't just that he could tell them exactly where they were at all times; it was also that he was able to mess with their minds in a way that created a sense of panic and confusion.

That was second nature to the fingersmith, of course. The power of misdirection and of making sure a subject's attention was on something other than her surroundings was something he knew well, and he had practiced it for many hours.

Sleight of hand was what it was. And this was the mental equivalent.

The only thing that was slightly disappointing to him was the thought that she might not have died. That was troubling him, and he knew he needed to give the process more thought.

First, though, he needed to focus on the next victim. Who would it be? He needed to find someone who was vulnerable, someone who was easily manipulated.

Looking around the mall, he realized that his powers were growing because he seemed to be able to pinpoint likely targets more easily. Almost the moment he looked up, he saw someone who would work.

That woman, there.

She was walking through the mall, head down, eyes averted, not wanting strangers to be part of her world, not interested in engaging with her environment. He watched her look warily at an oncoming man and step aside to avoid him.

All these physical tells were like gold to him. Pure gold! This was going to be a hugely successful target. She felt threatened by the world. Imagine how threatened she would feel by him. He could see she would easily panic. And then, he'd have her.

As he stood up and got ready to make his approach, drawing a deep breath and letting it out to contain his energy and make himself invisible, he wondered if, through his texts, he could start to influence where they went.

Making them make these terrible errors of judgment was wonderful in itself. But would it be possible to choose where they went, to make one of them climb out of the window of a skyscraper if he created enough of a sense of threat? How about messaging another while she was at the wheel of her car? That might be exciting, to force her to send the car slewing into other vehicles as she battled to escape someone she believed was chasing her.

Or else – or else, an even darker conclusion was coming to him. Something that was beckoning in his mind, an idea so perfectly tempting he couldn't deny it.

What if he followed the next one and killed her himself?

He let out a long breath, allowing excitement to flare. He thought the time was right for that. That he'd grown enough in his power to be able to do this.

It all started with planting the device. First things first, he reminded himself.

Once that was done, the seeds of his power could take root.

He walked swiftly up to her and withdrew his presence, and that little air tag slipped, ever so casually, into the side pocket of her purse where she would never, ever notice it.

He turned away, his movements calm, relaxed, and it was done. The tag was planted. The deed was done.

Should he wait a little?

He mused over that for a while, considering his options. He might need to wait for a little, just to let the heady triumph from his last successful mission ebb away.

After all, he didn't want to become careless or let any targeting go other than perfectly. The fingersmith knew that when it came to creating illusions, perfection was what was required, and nothing less would do.

Besides, she was prowling up and down the mall, probably trying to do some shopping, and it would be better to start the barrage of texts when she was somewhere more isolated. Somewhere that he would have the opportunity to do what he'd thought about.

He could wait. He could be patient and make sure it was the right time.

That was where it had gone wrong with the victim yesterday. He'd been too impatient, started texting her at the wrong time, and then she'd gotten home and into the protection of someone who'd been able to fight his techniques. So now he knew it was very important not to let these women connect with others who could help them.

The texts had to come thick and fast and threatening, and at a time when they were alone, and they were near somewhere dangerous.

And then, if he worded them right, this woman would be in his power.

He would own her; he would guide her. He would be in her mind.

And if she didn't end up killing herself, he would follow her and make her die.

CHAPTER TWENTY TWO

"I can't believe it!" Cami said aloud. "This guy, what he's been doing - it's chilling."

She reread the string of texts. Even though she didn't consider herself to be a very fearful or paranoid person, there was something about them that triggered that. For sure.

"He's inside her head. He's managed to hypnotize her, and she doesn't even know it. Now he's seeing what she's seeing," Cami read aloud. "He's channeling dark forces from beyond the grave, and she will now be haunted. If she blocks these texts, he'll find another way to get to her. She's his now."

"That's very disturbing," Connor agreed. As soon as they'd gotten the number, he'd gone and checked all the information on the burner phone while Cami had compiled the texts.

Unfortunately, like the other, it was turned off. Connor had traced the number and found that it had been sold through a different kiosk in a small center downtown.

As Cami had suspected, it was one stolen phone per victim. A cutoff loop again.

"You can see how those messages would push someone over the edge if they read it at the wrong time," Cami said. "He's describing her surroundings, in detail, in some of the texts. It really does sound as if he's walking beside her, or 'in her head' as he wants her to think. He must have maps and street views ready, as well as a lot of information on her. And he keeps reminding her that something's going to happen soon. That her time is limited. That he's about to take over, to confront her, that this is going to be going very bad, very fast."

Cami took in a deep breath. This was horrible to read. It was chilling and very disturbing.

"I can see why she did what she did. To have all these texts come in so fast and hard, it would create a sense of panic."

Connor nodded. "Yes. So, how can we tell how he's doing it? Where he's operating from?"

"It must be close to here," Cami said. "These women have been living their lives here, doing their shopping, going about their

95

business." She glanced again at the phone. The only intact phone they'd gotten. "Connor, you know what I've just thought?"

"What?" His tone reflected her own excitement.

"I've just thought that I can look back at Mindy's check-ins. I think they'd be visible on her phone. We could see where she went. And if we track her movements, back we might just work out that moment where he physically connected with her."

"What's the timeframe?" Connor asked.

"I think we're going back a day or two at most. I mean, she might pick a different coat; she might empty out her purse. I think that once he gets the tracker in there, he'll want to use it within a day. Those messages, so fast, so closely timed. He doesn't want to wait."

"That makes sense to me," Connor said. "So, what do we have?"

"I'm looking," Cami said.

She scrolled back through the activities and check-ins. She saw that Mindy worked as an attendant at a bus transportation company. Shift work, varying times. She'd been on shift quite a lot over the last few days. But when had she been off shift?

This morning, she'd been off, obviously. Cami didn't know where she'd been going. And yesterday afternoon, she'd just come off duty after a very long shift that had taken her out of town for a couple of days.

"It has to be yesterday," she said. "Yesterday was when this happened."

So, what were Mindy's check-ins?

She'd gone to the gym in the morning. Cami was hopeful about that until she saw that the gym was a ladies' only place with small classes. Unless this killer was extremely sneaky and had gotten very lucky with those class sizes and was pretending to be a man in the messages, the gym was out.

Cami was going to go with the more logical assumption that the killer was really a man and that that text reflected a truthful and disturbing glee.

"It's not the gym," she said.

"From there?"

"She went to the mall," Cami observed. "She often goes to a mall called Pine Ridge Center. It's her local mall. It's local to this area. She was there quite late, in the very late afternoon. I'm guessing after her trip out of town, she might have been picking up some groceries. But that's looking to me like the only place he could have got to her."

She locked eyes with Connor.

The local mall.

Now, finally, they were getting a solid lead.

"It makes sense because all the incidents and deaths have happened so close by," Cami said. Can we check up if the other victims used that mall? We can't see their check-ins, but maybe Vicky's housemates would know?"

"I'm going to give Grace a call straight away," Connor said, referring to his case notes.

A moment later, he was on the phone to Grace.

"It's FBI agent Connor here," he introduced himself quickly. "I have one more question for you that I'm hoping you'll be able to help me with. We need to know if Vicky shopped at a local mall called Pine Ridge Center?"

"Pine Ridge?" Listening closely, Cami heard Grace repeat the words. "Yes, we all shop there. They have a very good mix of stores. It's like a one-stop, especially in the winter when it's so cold," she said.

"Would she have been there in the past few days? Specifically, the day before her death or the day of her death?"

There was a thoughtful silence.

"Yes," Grace said. "She would have gone there because she was picking some work clothes up from the dry cleaners before heading into the office. So she went there on the morning of her death."

"Thank you very much," Connor said.

With that confirmed, they hustled to the car. Cami knew they wouldn't end up getting three out of three because Pippa's locations couldn't be confirmed on her damaged phone, and she lived alone. But two out of three, confirmed, was enough to make it a certainty.

The next stop was Pine Ridge Center, and now they were sure that it was the killer's hunting ground. It wasn't far away and would have been easily accessible for all three of the victims so far.

"You have been here before?" Connor asked as they joined the queue to get into the parking lot. Already, mid-morning, this mall was busy and popular. It was clearly a destination for locals.

"I haven't, actually. It's too far out of my orbit," Cami admitted.

"Mine, too," Connor agreed. "Close, but not close enough."

So that characterized this center. It was truly a local mall that attracted most of its shoppers from a fairly narrow catchment area. This killer might even live near here, Cami guessed, and he had used a familiar space as his hunting ground.

Then, another logical leap connected in her mind.

"If he lives near here, and he has stalked the women from here because they all live nearby and use this mall, then I wonder if he purchased the air tags from here, too? Maybe there's a place here that sells those white tags?"

She scrambled out of the car as soon as Connor had parked, leading the way inside, now feeling intent on seeing if her theory was correct.

Not just air tags but ones that looked specifically like the tags that the killer had planted on his victims. They were unusual. Not branded, not colorful, and perhaps they were all from a certain batch of merchandise that someone in the mall had gotten in for sale.

A glance at the store directory allowed her to narrow down the options of stores that might sell them. There were three. The phone shop to the right, the big electronics store down the main aisle, and a small gadget and novelty shop right at the end.

Cami and Connor set out on the hunt.

A quick foray around the phone shop showed Cami that although they did sell air tags, they were only the branded items. There weren't any of the unusual white ones there.

"Next stop?" she said to Connor. That was the electronics store.

Walking in there, Cami took her time, knowing that they might stock a few different brands and that she'd need to look through all the options to make sure.

She walked around, taking in what was there, assessing whether there was anything similar, while Connor waited at the door.

She returned to him shaking her head.

"Nothing, yet," she said.

But the final shop, all the way at the far end of the mall, might possibly be the best bet, Cami thought. After all, it was a novelty and gadget shop and sold unusual items.

It was their last chance, and she felt determined that if there were air tags there, she was going to sniff them out.

She headed into the shop.

The assistant, sitting at the desk on the far end, was a young woman with bobbed hair cut squarely and pale olive skin. She didn't even look up as Cami and Connor walked in. Cami went straight to the shelves, looking through the merchandise. Connor walked up to speak to the woman herself.

"Help you?" she asked.

"I'm looking for air tags," Connor replied.

"We got a whole heap of those," she said. "My boss is really into all this tracking and remote locating. He's quite passionate about it."

"He is?" Cami listened harder to this conversation. This could be very important information. The boss clearly wasn't here now. He'd left the store in the assistant's hands. Where was he? Out tracking more victims?

"Yes. He's really into being able to remotely monitor people and things and to remotely communicate as if you were there. He thinks it's an amazing tool. I guess it's very useful for catching criminals, too," she said to Connor, who was making interesting noises and asking her more questions about her boss. Cami guessed Connor was thinking exactly the same as her. This boss was a possible suspect. It sounded like he had a passionate interest in these devices. Maybe even an obsessive interest.

As they conversed, Cami walked along the rows of merchandise to the section where the air tags were displayed.

She felt a chill as she saw them.

There were a few different and unusual types of air tags here, and immediately her gaze was drawn to a pack of them that were identical to the two she'd gotten from the victims. Plain white, waterproof, high quality, and way more expensive than the ones in the other stores. These were premium items. Without a doubt, they'd been bought here. Or maybe not bought, Cami revised as Connor continued his conversation. Maybe the store owner had just used them.

Connor looked around, and Cami was able to give him a decisive nod. Now, he had a yes and could continue with his very productive line of questioning.

She sidled up, standing next to him but not intruding on the conversation as she didn't want the dynamic between Connor and the saleswoman to be disturbed right now.

"Can you tell me, do you keep a record of who buys them?" Connor asked.

"No, we don't do that," the woman said. Now she'd started to look worried as if she was starting to realize that Connor wasn't asking about these items because he wanted to buy some but because there was trouble afoot.

"Look, I don't really feel authorized to tell you anything more," she said nervously. "Can you rather speak to my boss? Here's his card. He went out just now, but he must still be in the mall, as his car keys are still here."

"Thank you," Connor said.

They turned and walked out of the store.

"So," Connor said as soon as he was around the corner and out of sight of the gadget store. "That was an interesting conversation. We now know that the store owner seems to love these tags, that he's very into the idea of tracking people, and this is the only store that sells the ones we need. So I think before we go any further, we should do some more research on the owner himself." He looked down at the business card. "Patrick Potts. Let's find out if Patrick Potts's interest in these devices, and in tracking people, has ever extended to breaking the law."

They moved to the side of the corridor, standing in a quiet corner of the mall, and Connor got on his phone.

"I'm calling to find out about a record," he said when the person on the other end picked up, and Cami's eyes flew wide.

A record? Could Patrick Potts have an actual record?

It turned out to be yes.

Connor hung up and turned to her.

"Patrick Potts has a history of harassment," he said. "He's had charges laid against him three times for harassing and following female coworkers at his previous jobs, as well as an ex-girlfriend. He paid a fine and served a suspended sentence two years ago. It seems like he might be our man. And if he's somewhere in this mall, we need to find him, fast."

CHAPTER TWENTY THREE

"We need to track his phone," Cami said to Connor. She stared around the mall, feeling intent and alert and as if they were just moments away from catching him.

He might be here, now, in this mall. If Patrick Potts was their killer, he probably was here.

Cami's theory was that he was leaving his store in the assistant's hands while he went out to follow his compulsion for tracking people.

Connor sighed. "Unfortunately, there's no cellphone number on this business card. It's the store number only. I think that assistant felt that we might want to contact him via email because that's the only other information here."

"Oh, no," she said. She'd been ready to give tracking a go with a brand new program that would work especially well if the target phone was close by.

"So, seeing we can't track his phone, we can at least look for him. Thanks to the record, there's a very clear description of him on file, and that's coming through now," Connor said calmly. "Let's wait until we have that and then go physically searching for him."

Cami nodded. The old-fashioned way was winning the day again. Technology couldn't always work, and now it would be boots on the ground and eyes searching. She hoped she'd be able to spot him and that she'd be able to prove herself in something she knew wasn't her area of expertise.

"Well, here's the description," Connor said. He immediately shared the physical description and the photo with Cami. As soon as her phone beeped, she opened it and stared down at the man, looking at his brooding face, his hooded eyes, his intense expression. He had a mass of dark, spiky hair and three earrings in his left ear. He looked older than his thirty-five years to her, and she thought he looked like someone who could easily have decided to stalk and harass his victims with terrible threats.

They walked through the mall, looking carefully to the left and right, keeping an eye out for all the public places where their suspect might be sitting.

Cami kept the picture of the man's face fixed in her mind as she walked, carefully looking at everyone he saw, hoping that she'd spot that lean, long face and the man's demeanor that she thought would look furtive and wary. At any rate, the picture, though a moment in time, had seemed to suggest that.

She stared around, seeking the demeanor as much as she was seeking the looks. Looking for someone with that angle to his head, who'd probably be slinking along, looking out of the corners of his own eyes at people while he avoided eye contact with others.

Where would he be? The coffee shops and restaurants provided the most obvious places for people-watching, but he might also be sneakily waiting in a clothing store. Brushing past someone who was heading for a changing room with an armful of clothes to try on would be a good way to slip that air tag into a pocket unnoticed. So Cami was paying particular attention to the clothing stores as she passed them.

But it was Connor who suddenly stopped, grasping her arm quickly as he stared to the right.

"Cami, I've seen him," he said. "We need to move in. He's at the coffee shop, but he's paid, and he's standing up. We must get him before he goes."

Cami spun around. And as she did, she saw the man's head jerk sideways, looking at both of them. It was weirdly as if he'd sensed their stares, and that had attracted him to them.

He stared back at them with a long, dark look.

Then, Connor was hustling toward the entrance to the coffee shop, clearly not wanting to get involved in another chase down.

"Patrick Potts? Is that you, sir? FBI here," he asked, striding up to the table.

The man stared at him, an inscrutable expression, for a long moment. Cami felt her stomach clench even though she didn't even know exactly why. It was something to do with the intent in that gaze. Something about it was chilling. If she'd had the chance to read his thoughts right now, she wouldn't have wanted to because she sensed that they were cold and dark.

And then, as he stared at them, he began to laugh. A grating, mirthless laugh that went on and on. He laughed as Connor reached him, and he laughed when Connor showed him his badge.

"I need you to come with us," Connor told him.

At that point, the man stopped laughing, and now, Cami could see something lurking in his eyes that she didn't like at all.

"Think very carefully before you bring me in," he threatened. "I will not play your little games. I'm done with police, and I'm done with your attempts to convict me."

"We need to talk to you about the air tags sold in your store. If you can give us what we need cooperatively, it shouldn't take long. Please, come with us," Connor said, being friendly and persuasive even though Cami was sure that a short conversation wasn't likely.

Another deep, antagonistic stare.

And then, the man's fists moved faster than Cami had even thought possible. They flew back and lashed forward, and she gasped because Connor was directly in the path of a brutal punch.

Only he wasn't. Connor ducked aside in one smooth movement so that Patrick's fist skimmed past him and, instead of crashing into his face, simply glanced off his shoulder. And while it did, Connor twisted around and grabbed the man's arm, pulling it sideways in a move that didn't look fast but was somehow massively unbalancing, so that Patrick staggered forward. He flung out his other arm to save himself, and it slammed down onto the table. The milk jug overturned, splashing white liquid onto the checked cloth, and the cup smashed down onto the floor. Around them, there was a commotion as frightened shoppers scattered, jumping up from their tables, cringing away to avoid what seemed like the start of a violent fight. Only Cami could see that the fight was already contained and that Connor was ready for whatever Patrick might try.

The waitresses scattered, but with a confident swagger, the young manager left the front desk and rushed over, helping Connor, grasping Patrick's other arm firmly.

"Whatever you're doing here, sir, I'll help you out," he said. "I'm sure we can handle this calmly. Can we get this customer off the premises for the time being?"

He looked down at the smashed cup, clearly wanting no more of the same in his shop.

"I'm sure we can, and thank you," Connor said. He turned to Patrick.

"Seems you don't want to talk?" Connor asked. The man was still trying to twist out of his grasp, but now that the manager had his other arm, Cami could see his efforts were futile. The two men were grasping him firmly, and Connor still had him off balance.

"You think I'll talk to you outside? You're wrong about that. So wrong," Patrick jeered.

"In that case, we'll talk in the FBI offices. Come with me. Now. If you play nice, I won't handcuff you. But one more attempt at a punch from you, and I will."

Patrick had stopped struggling. He'd submitted to Connor's grasp. And he submitted to being led across the restaurant, with Connor and the manager both holding tightly to his arms.

But the expression in his eyes hadn't changed, and he stared at Connor with a narrowed gaze that chilled Cami to the bone.

"Bring me in," he said. "I'll come with you. I won't try to escape you. But I warn you right now, I'm not going to play nice."

CHAPTER TWENTY FOUR

So far, Patrick Potts had been truthful about one thing, Cami thought ruefully, shifting on her cold, steel chair. And that was that he wasn't going to play nice. He hadn't been playing nice.

As soon as Connor had seated him in the interrogation room, handcuffed to the steel table, his attitude had shifted from cold and silent to aggressive and hostile. He had refused to answer any questions and had made it clear that he wasn't going to cooperate in any way.

Cami watched as Connor tried to reason with him, but it was clear that the man was going to use this opportunity not to answer any questions but simply to give them his thoughts on law enforcement while they waited for his lawyer to arrive.

Of course, he'd insisted on a lawyer. This man knew his rights, and he was exercising them. But why would this all be necessary, she wondered, if he was innocent?

Did he not realize that his behavior was showing them clearly he had something to hide?

"You guys, you're on some kind of power trip," Patrick spat out. "That's what this is all about, isn't it?"

"We simply need information," Connor said calmly. Cami admired his self-control and polite tone, especially after he'd narrowly avoided a potentially lethal punch. Connor's cat-quick reflexes were paired with a very resilient temperament, she realized. Something for her to emulate. Holding grudges didn't work when it came to interrogations.

"Why should I spill anything out to you? Give me one reason why I should do that?"

"It'll go better if you cooperate with the police. It always makes things easier," Connor said. "After all, you keep telling us you're innocent of the crimes. So now's your chance to prove it."

He stared at them. Then he began to laugh again, a weird, cold, humorless sound.

"You want me to do your job for you?" he asked.

"I want you to tell the truth," Connor said firmly. "And if you've got nothing to hide, then that shouldn't be a problem. All we need from you is some information on your whereabouts at certain times, the existence of an alibi, and also more information on those air tags and who bought them."

Patrick sneered at him. "Innocent until proven guilty, right? Except you guys are trying to prove me guilty without any evidence. You just want to pin this on me because it's convenient for you."

"We have evidence that the air tags that were planted on the victims of these crimes were sold in your shop. Now, unfortunately, you have a record of similar offenses," Connor said. "Therefore, if you're not guilty, a reasonable man would be looking to provide us with evidence that proves it. It's got to be better than sitting in a cell, right?"

Patrick's eyes gleamed with a momentary triumph.

"You'll never be able to prove it," he said. "I'm not the only one selling those things, you know."

Cami discreetly scrolled through her phone, looking for the description that the cellphone store owner had given the police about the stolen phones. She thought that description matched this man well. He was even wearing a gray jacket now, just like the one that the store owner had described. It didn't have a hood, though. The thief in the store had a hood.

Having confirmed that for herself, she tuned back into the conversation.

"In this mall, you are the only seller of them. It's probably the only place in the neighborhood that sells this particular type of items," Connor insisted. "But maybe you're completely innocent and just angry at the police for inconveniencing you. In that case, all you have to do is to let us know if you kept any records of those air tag sales. They're unusual items and quite expensive. Maybe you or your assistant remembered?"

"You can't get that information from me. I protect my customers against bullying from the police. It's an added service, you could say. And in any case, people are allowed to use my air tags any way they want." His eyes narrowed. "If they are clever enough to use those tags in a way that brings them some amusement, then who am I to stop them?"

"Where were you this morning, at about eight a.m.?"

"Somewhere you don't need to know about," the man said, with cunning in every word. "I'm not going to tell you until my lawyer gets here because I don't need you to trap me."

At that point, Connor stood up.

"We'll be back, Mr. Potts. And you, for now, are staying here."

A flash of anger crossed the man's lean, sneering face. But Connor ignored it. He stood up and walked out with Cami following.

"Any update on his phone?" Connor asked as soon as they had walked down the corridor to a safe distance away from the interview room.

Cami nodded. "There might be. Let me check." Patrick had refused to open his phone at all, stating his right to privacy and that he wasn't going to do a thing without his lawyer there. She was running a hack on it via her laptop that would get through - she was confident of it - but it would take time. The phone and laptop were squirreled away on a desk in an office down the corridor from the interview room. Now, she headed hopefully into the room and took a look.

No progress as yet. Her program was running, trying every quick fix and combination at lightning speed, but it just wasn't in yet.

"It might take another hour or two," Cami said. "I'm really sorry. I wish this was one of the times I could make it happen quickly, but it happens to be a model with no easy hacks into it."

She felt so frustrated at her lack of progress.

"I'm wondering how much information we'll get off it anyway," Connor said. "The phones that were used in these crimes were different phones, burner items, that were used and then thrown away. He might have done the tracking on those throwaway devices, too, to be extra secure. If he's got something on his phone he doesn't want us to see; it could be unrelated to this."

"No," Cami said. "Those air tags would have to be activated by an iPhone at least. Even if they were tracked via another phone. But personally, I feel iPhone to iPhone would be the quickest and most reliable."

"And he has an iPhone," Connor stated. "However, we have to keep in mind that he could be trying to keep something totally different from us. Guilty behavior doesn't necessarily mean guilty of the crime we'd like them to be convicted for. The lawyer can apparently only get here after lunch, so until then, we're going to be going around in circles, and I'm wondering if there's a better way to do this."

Cami nodded. "Yes. I was wondering if it would be worth going back and speaking to that store assistant. She might just remember if anyone bought a few of those air tags at one time."

"That's an idea," Connor said. "But I think she might have the same attitude to law enforcement as her boss."

"She won't talk to you," Cami agreed. But a theory was starting to form in her mind. "What if she talks to me? I don't think she really saw or noticed me with you because she was so focused on you. And I was wearing my baseball cap. I could go back into the mall on my own and without my FBI jacket and cap on. I could wear a normal jacket instead. Nobody expects to see this hairstyle under the cap," she added, brushing her hand over the shaven side.

Connor nodded.

"I think that's our best plan. At this moment, he hasn't had the chance to call his assistant, and she doesn't yet know he's been arrested, although she might suspect something's wrong. But yes, I think now's about as good a time as we're going to get," he said.

"I'll take a cab there right now. And I'll call you when I have any results. I'll try my best to get something from her," Cami said. "Even if it's a lead as to what Patrick's really doing, it might give us more information you can use. And there must be a chance she remembers something if she was at the till when someone came through and bought those tags. Maybe, if Patrick isn't the criminal, she might remember more about the man who is?"

Connor nodded. "You've got a lot to do, Cami. And I can't come with you. I need to keep chipping away at this man, and if his lawyer arrives early, then we'll need to head straight into that session with him." He paused, looking at her worriedly. "Please, be careful."

"I will," she promised, hearing the seriousness in his tone.

But Connor wasn't done yet.

"I want you to call me, or call my office if you suspect anything at all is wrong. Remember, if the man we're looking for is not sitting in the interrogation room, then he's out there and dangerous. He uses the mall as his hunting ground. And if he suspects he's being hunted in turn, then he might try to protect himself in whatever way he can."

CHAPTER TWENTY FIVE

Cami felt nervous but resolute as she climbed out of the cab at the Pine Ridge Mall's entrance. This was her chance to try to get some valuable information on the case. If she did things right, then she might get them closer to this killer.

The more she thought about it, the more she felt in two minds about Patrick Potts being the actual killer.

Sure, he might be, but the way he'd been hedging when Connor asked those questions, it was like he was just buying time.

Maybe Patrick was guilty of something else.

Maybe he knew the killer and was protecting him because he was a good source of sales for those air tags that were priced higher than the average for those items. There were all sorts of reasons why he might be refusing to answer these questions.

Even now, the killer might be at the mall, watching out for more victims. It gave her a very uneasy feeling to think that he might be here, on the prowl, looking out for women who fitted his evil agenda. Maybe even watching her.

A thought occurred to Cami, sudden and surprising.

Could she set herself up as a potential victim?

As she entered the mall's warm, noisy environment, with shopping carts rattling and kids squealing and footsteps clattering, Cami wondered about that.

Would it be possible that she could play the role and be targeted herself?

She gave it some very long and hard consideration before deciding the answer was no.

She looked too different and unusual, and especially now, with her baseball cap removed and her trendy hairstyle showing, and her sky blue jacket on in place of the navy FBI issue garment, and her Docs. The women who the killer had targeted hadn't had tattoos or edgy hairstyles. They had been more conservative in their dress and demeanor, less out there. She didn't fit his type, and she couldn't make herself into that type. Unfortunately.

So, with that ruled out, it was time to go and confront the saleswoman in the gadget shop.

As she walked through the mall, she kept her eyes peeled for anything suspicious, looking for someone who might fit the profile of the killer, or at any rate, the little they knew about him.

There was the shop ahead. And there was the assistant, sitting at the desk, scrolling through her phone. Cami noted that she looked bored, but that was good, right? Looking bored was better than looking worried. If she looked worried, then all her defenses would be up.

Cami sauntered into the shop, hoping to keep the atmosphere relaxed because she needed her to be unwary if she was going to get answers.

She was glad to see that the woman didn't recognize her in the slightest. It was amazing, Cami thought. Wearing the FBI cap and jacket, people saw only what they represented and didn't really take note of the person inside the clothing at all.

No cameras in the store, she saw. Not visible ones, anyway. In a gadget shop like this, there might be a hidden one, but it was such a tiny store that she couldn't stand in the middle of it and start searching for wifi signals that might point the way.

Even so, she didn't go straight to the counter but browsed around the shop, taking a look at the merchandise. It would be a good idea to buy something, she thought. That would give her a better start than simply marching up and asking questions. And this shop had some very cool merchandise. Cami was immediately taken by a cellphone case that was black in color, with miniature silver cats on it. That was something she needed, for sure, and it was available in her phone's model. And should she buy Kieran something?

Cami's gaze fell on a tiny speaker in the shape of a miniature Jack Daniels bottle. That was really cute. Kieran was a Jack Daniels drinker; she'd seen a bottle in the cupboard in the kitchen. And those speakers were a brand she knew was good quality.

With her two purchases in hand, she headed over, wondering what the best way to embark on this conversation would be.

The woman put down her phone and stared at Cami, still bored, still not recognizing her.

"This speaker, is it good quality?" she asked.

She pushed over a few ten-dollar bills to make payment, wanting to see how the cash sale was recorded.

"It's very good quality," the woman said. She seemed in a bad mood and kept glancing down at her phone. As she jotted down the price of the item, Cami stole a look at her phone's screen.

She appeared to be having an argument with her boyfriend about whether he was allowed to go out with his friends tonight. There was no darker reason for her being angry.

And she wasn't even scanning the items! She was just jotting down the price and adding it up with her phone's calculator. The cash sales were off the books for sure, Cami realized. She guessed that was one of the things that Patrick Potts didn't want anyone to know about, and it made their job much more difficult.

"I read online about an air tag that someone said they bought from this store," she said. "Are those good quality?"

"They're the best. Good quality, but more expensive than normal. Very accurate and waterproof, and the battery lasts," she said.

"Have you sold a lot recently?" Cami asked.

"We sell them all the time, but I haven't been here recently. I've been on vacation," she said abruptly. "This is my first day back."

She said it like it wasn't a good thing.

"Your boss works here the rest of the time?"

She grimaced. "Yeah. He's breathing down my neck the whole time in this shop. I don't know where he is now, he might have gone out to get coffee and order stock, but he's not usually away for so long. He'll be back and probably mad at me for even talking to you."

She made a face that told Cami clearly that she hated her life. Then she pushed her change across the counter. Cami guessed no cash receipt would be forthcoming, and she didn't ask for one. This was how they did things here.

Taking her purchases, she turned away. This outing had proved to be nothing but a disaster. The woman who might have seen something had been on vacation, and also, it was even clearer that the store owner spent a lot of time in his shop, micromanaging his environment. That meant he wasn't out in the mall, looking for people to plant air tags on and tracking their movements.

It was even less likely that Patrick Potts was their culprit, and although she was sure he knew who'd been buying a lot of the air tags, she was equally sure he wouldn't tell them because he hated the police and he also didn't want his own misdoings exposed. Among these was a level of tax evasion she already saw.

Cami left the store with her purchases, feeling frustrated.

If only she'd been able to do better. Now she was heading back to Connor with a big fat zero in terms of her progress. All she'd done was to probably rule out their suspect in custody.

She wasn't ready to go back yet. Instead, Cami decided to take one last walk through the mall. There might be something that she could pick up on. There might be some glimpse of the killer. Maybe if she spotted a likely-looking woman, someone he might target, she could follow her for a little while and see if anyone brushed up against her or planted one of those tags.

She knew this idea was extremely unlikely to succeed but doggedly decided to give it some time anyway.

Walking along the passages and corridors, she took a look around. Outside of the mall's main corridor, where the high street, mainstream stores were located, there were warrens of smaller and more interesting shops. There was a second-hand bookshop where she'd have loved to have spent some time. There was a tattoo and piercing studio that seemed to produce fabulous work from a look at the photos outside.

And what was this ahead? All the way down this narrow corridor? Now this was interesting.

In fact, as she saw the sign, Cami started to wonder if it would be worth looking at it more closely.

"The Guru's Grotto. Palm Reading – Future Predictions - Hypnosis - Tarot Readings. We can Predict your Life Course and Influence your Future," the sign boasted. *"Allow us to Walk With you on your Life Journey and Guide you to the Positives."*

It wasn't the sign itself so much as the language used, Cami thought. In a weird way, it was echoing what she'd read in those text messages sent to the women. There was a similarity there, in the thinking, in the communication style.

Not until now had she wondered whether this killer might actually be a tenant at the mall. What if he might actually have a business here, and that was why he was able to spend all day, every day here?

It would be better to go back to Connor with some answers, or at least a new direction, than with nothing at all.

Deciding this was worth looking into, Cami squared her shoulders and walked into the dimly lit environment, with a jangling bell announcing her arrival as she pushed open the door to the Guru's Grotto.

CHAPTER TWENTY SIX

Cami had never been in a place like the Guru's Grotto before. Mind readings? Hypnosis? She had no similar experiences to compare it with, and to her, this musty-smelling interior felt creepy. She'd have been far more at ease in the tattoo parlor, back down the corridor. Now, she felt all the way out of her comfort zone as she headed inside, wondering if there were going to be clues to be found.

How would she get those clues? What would she even ask for to provide a reason for coming inside this space as a newcomer to this world?

Was this the norm, she wondered, staring around at the walls - painted dark red and dark blue, with some of the symbols that she vaguely associated with tarot card readings.

The ceiling was painted black. A glass-fronted cabinet at the far side of the small room held a few crystals, some amulets, some essential oils, and a few pieces of silver and platinum jewelry. On the wall shelves were other items. An incense burner, a ceremonial dagger, some bowls and statuettes.

There was a small table next to the cabinet. It was unoccupied, but as she began rethinking the wisdom of this decision and turned around, a door behind the table opened. It had been almost invisible in that blue-painted wall.

Hurriedly, she turned back, feeling her pulse speed up.

"Good morning," a man said, walking in. He looked to be in his late twenties, with brown hair cut short and a pale face, wearing a pair of deep gray pants and a black fleece top.

"Morning," Cami said, still at a loss. Was this the psychic? She needed to think of some questions to ask him, and fast.

But the man soon corrected her thinking.

"If you're here to see our Guru, he's just finishing up with a hypnosis client. What would you like to book in for?"

Cami hesitated. "What are the options?" she asked, playing for time.

"Our Guru can help you with whatever you need," the man said calmly. "You can have a hypnosis session, past life regression, reiki healing, a crystal reading, a tarot reading, a palm reading, or else a simple consultation to work out your needs."

"I think the consultation sounds good," Cami said. She was still staring around like a tourist who'd just been teleported to an unfamiliar location. She knew she should be more inscrutable and stop rubbernecking, but this was so weird.

"Please, take a seat," the man said, ushering her over to a chair. "Tea? Coffee?"

"I'm fine, thanks," Cami said. She was starting to feel nervous. She should be checking in with Connor again and not sitting here, waiting for a consultation on a whim. How long would this hypnosis session even take? What if the Guru was going to be tied up for another hour?

As she sat there, waiting for the hypnosis session to finish, Cami tried to calm her misgivings and focus her thoughts. She needed to come up with a plan, a way to find out if someone here was behind the murders. Maybe this place held some answers, and if so, then she would need to ask the right questions. She glanced around the dimly lit room again, taking in the symbols and trinkets adorning the walls.

And then, the man returned, snapping Cami out of her thoughts. "Our Guru is ready to see you now," he said, gesturing towards the door at the back of the room."

He opened the door. Inside, it was even darker. Cami smelled the fragrance of incense and saw a table, with a candle burning in a candelabra in its center.

She walked through, ushered again by the assistant, and as her eyes adjusted to the gloom and the flickering flame, she made out the face of the man sitting beyond.

He was an older man, in his fifties, she guessed. He said nothing for a while but stared at her with narrowed eyes.

She realized the door behind her had closed. So soundlessly that she hadn't even heard. Now, she was alone in here with him.

How had she gotten into this, she wondered, with a flare of panic.

His voice was soft and steady.

"Sit down, please," he said. "Sit in the chair. Collect your thoughts. I can see you are disturbed. Look at the way the candle flame is flickering, even though there is no breeze in here. It's picking up on your thoughts. In here, it's easy for the forces from beyond to tune into your mind."

This was sounding suspiciously similar to those messages, Cami thought with a shiver.

She sat down, looking at this man. It was difficult to see his face clearly, but those eyes gleamed. He wore a gray, hooded garment, but she couldn't see if it was a jacket or a cloak.

"I sense that you are in search of something," the guru said, his voice low and hypnotic. "Something that you cannot find on your own."

Cami felt a chill run down her spine. How did he know? Was he really psychic? Or was he just adept at reading people and playing on their desires and fears?

"I'm looking for answers," she said, trying to keep her voice steady.

The guru nodded slowly. "And what is it that you need answers to?"

"I guess - um - career direction," she said.

He laughed. It was a soft, sibilant sound. "No, you don't. You don't need that at all. My spirits are telling me clearly. You know your abilities, and you know your direction. You don't need my advice on that at all. Why would you come in here just to lie? Are you not ready to face the truth? So I ask you again - why are you here, with your disturbed thoughts, making my flame dance and sputter?"

This was all too weird for her.

She should ask this man if he'd ever followed anyone. If he'd ever tracked anyone. She knew she should try to shock him with her questions, to try to get the truth out of him, but the problem was that he was too good at what he did. It really felt as if he could read her mind. It was intensely creepy.

"I strongly feel you've come in here for a reason. With a purpose. That you wanted to open yourself up to me and ask me something important. What is it, and are you going to ask it?" he pressured her.

"Uh - you know, I think I need some air," Cami said. She couldn't do anything with this man's gaze pinned on her. But what she had seen in the back of the room was the faint glow of a phone screen. He had his phone with him, and if she could log into this wifi, maybe she could get a glimpse of it. Maybe she could see if there were any air tags connected to it. But she couldn't do it here. She needed to get out of this back room, get some distance from him, and then log into his wifi and see what she could find.

And, call Connor. She needed to do that too. He needed to know that there was something here that wasn't right, that this man's pattern was disturbingly similar to the tone of the messages, and that they needed to bring this Guru in and question him.

"Can I have a moment?" she asked, gesturing to the door that was almost invisible in the wall.

"Sure," he said. "Take as long as you need. When you're ready to come in, I'll be waiting."

I'm sure you will, Cami thought, feeling goose bumps prickled her arms. I'm sure you will be waiting. But just don't read my mind in the meantime, okay?

Trying very hard not to think about what she was planning to do, in case this creepy and perceptive man read her body language, Cami got up and walked out.

As soon as she was out, she breathed in a deep, relieved breath. She had no idea where the assistant was, and the waiting room was empty, but now, she needed to get on to the wifi as soon as she could and before this guru started getting suspicious.

Perching on the chair she'd sat in previously, she began her job. Quickly, her hands unsteady with haste, she set her program to run.

She needed to get into his phone to see if this creepy guru was hiding anything, and if ever there was a time when the wifi needed to give her results fast, that time was now.

Cami gabbled a prayer to herself as she let it run, sending good vibes, speedy vibes because she'd only have a few minutes before he would come out to look for her.

She glanced at her screen and let out a sigh of relief.

The program had worked. She was in.

And now, to hunt through the phone itself.

CHAPTER TWENTY SEVEN

Here it was. On the wifi, Cami could now see the other devices connected, and the one she needed was there. This was a race against time. She knew she had only minutes to get into it and try to find what she needed, but at least the first step was taken.

"iPhone", and the model. She could see it on the network.

Although, wait. Here was another, which had just popped up, a slightly earlier model. So there were two. He had two phones? Was one a burner? How did this work?

She'd just need to search both as fast as she could. And she decided to start with the earlier one, just because she'd get quicker access to the section of the phone she wanted. And that was the tracking of the airbags.

She was sure it had been done from an iPhone. And the burner phones, the ones that had been stolen from the shop and used to send the texts, had not been iPhones. So he'd used a more powerful phone, and one that could interact with the air tag software, to set them up at least.

Now, to see if the air tags were visible on this phone.

"Okay," she muttered. "Let's go."

She could see something already. Narrowing down her search, navigating to a section of the phone that was luckily not too encrypted, she could see that a few different air tags had been logged into recently, and their movements had been tracked.

Frantically, because she knew that time was running short now, she looked to see when the last tracking had been done.

It was this morning. This morning, from seven a.m. to eight-thirty, an air tag had been tracked. That would coincide exactly with when poor Mindy Knowles had rushed into traffic in a terrified state.

There was another one from yesterday. Perhaps that had been an unsuccessful targeting, Cami theorized, or else he was still busy with her.

And the next most recent?

That was the day before yesterday, in the early evening, when Pippa had plummeted to her death. Both these trackings coincided to the minute with the two more recent victims.

And now, she saw that a new one was linked to it. A brand new one, activated just a few minutes earlier, was there, waiting, ready to be tracked. A new victim had been chosen as he continued with his evil game.

Cami didn't need to go back any further. She knew now that this was the right phone. Her instinct had been right. She had it.

Now, she needed to call Connor and fast. Because Connor could take this forward. All she had to do was try to make sure this creepy magician psychic person didn't figure out what she was doing and make a run for it.

But as she opened her phone's keyboard to make the call, a side door swung wide. Another invisible gap in the wall that she hadn't noticed before. Immediately, Cami lowered her phone, quickly palming it down by the side of her body, not wanting to be seen by the creepy magician.

But as the door opened wider, the assistant walked out of it.

He looked surprised to see her.

"Well, hello," he said. "You already finished?"

Cami shook her head. "I just came out to get some air, that's all," she said.

"Ah, I see. And to obviously use your phone?" He stared at her.

"What do you mean?" Cami said. There was something about the way he'd said this that was ringing alarm bells in her mind.

The way he'd said it, it almost sounded as if - as if he knew she'd been doing that. But she'd put the phone away as soon as that door had opened. How had he known?

Was he a mind reader too?

No. She didn't think so, not when there was an easier explanation.

The reason that was now occurring to her was that he'd seen her phone come up on the wifi network.

That meant he was using it too.

And now, Cami realized, with abrupt suddenness, that she'd been wrong. She'd been very wrong.

The newer phone belonged to the Guru himself.

And the older iPhone - well, that must belong to the assistant. And he'd just been connecting up online. He'd just been adding that air tag to his phone. If she didn't act fast, then he was going to use it, and another woman would be in terrible danger.

Right now, Cami was acutely aware that she was in danger, too. Did he know about her? Did he know who she was?

She didn't think so, but she couldn't tell from his face. He could just be hiding his thoughts. She needed to be very careful now.

If only she could call Connor, but she didn't want to do anything that might spook him.

"I was just checking a message quickly," she said.

The assistant raised his eyebrows but didn't say anything. Cami could feel his gaze on her like he was trying to read her mind. She clenched her fists, trying to keep her thoughts in check.

"Interesting that you were able to log into our wifi. I don't remember giving you the password," he said. He was staring at her intensely now. He was looking at her with suspicion written all over his face. For sure, he knew what she'd been doing. He knew.

Cami tried to keep her composure. "Oh, sorry, I just guessed it," she said, hoping it sounded convincing. "I'm pretty good with technology."

The assistant narrowed his eyes. "Is that so?" he said. "Well, I'm pretty good with people. And I'm getting the feeling that you're not who you say you are."

Now, Cami was realizing that his earlier calm attitude had been a front. That was starting to crumble, and from behind it, she could see a new man. The real man. He was emerging. And he was dangerous.

"Maybe you're wrong!" She raised her voice to a shout because she wanted the guru to hear that something scary and dangerous was playing out in his waiting room. Right now, she'd realized that the man she'd believed was creepy was actually the man she needed to come in here, so she could buy some time to get help. "Maybe I'm just a normal innocent woman who doesn't like being threatened!"

"How can you say that?" he answered, his voice also rising. "You logged into our wifi. What did you see there? What are you doing? You're not just a hacker, are you? You're here for another reason. And yes, I can tell!"

At that moment, what Cami had been hoping for occurred. The door in the dark blue wall burst open, and the guru stepped out, looking annoyed and confused. Cami was glad to see those emotions on his face because it hopefully meant he wasn't in league with this assistant.

"What's going on here?" he demanded. "Radzi, what is this about?"

119

"I'm having an argument with your assistant," Cami said. "And I'd like you please to monitor Radzi while I call the police."

"Radzi, what have you done? I want to mentor you the way you deserve. Don't let me down. Please be the person I believe you are," the guru pleaded, and Cami could hear a wealth of sadness and regret in the words. This hinted to her that the guru knew Radzi had done something wrong in the past and had hired him anyway. Maybe he'd believed in second chances.

Shaking his head, the guru turned to Cami.

"Call the police," he ordered in sorrowful tones. "I will watch him."

But that was the wrong word to say.

It was a triggering command.

With a cry of rage, Radzi leaped up and grabbed the ornamental dagger from the wall. He whipped it out of its scabbard and, with a cry of rage, plunged it straight into the guru's chest.

"No!" Cami screamed. She couldn't believe what was happening. The breath huffed out of her in an astonished gasp. She'd just watched this man stab - actually stab - his boss. The guru fell to his knees and then slumped to the ground, coughing weakly.

Cami didn't have time to see whether he was dead or alive because the assistant swung around to her.

Rage was in his eyes, and a bloody knife was clutched in his hand.

This had turned bad – deadly – in one short instant. Cami knew she had only a moment to get away.

She needed to run now, for her life.

CHAPTER TWENTY EIGHT

The fingersmith had spotted the young woman outside, and immediately, alarm bells had clamored in his mind. Of course, they had. The way she'd stared at the door, the way she'd looked around, fidgeting uneasily, but not in the same way that the Guru's customers, or potential customers, did.

He had seen enough of their approaches to that sacred door to know what normal behavior was like for a newbie wanting a consultation, and this wasn't it. This was something different. She was here for a different reason.

He could see it instantly, and he knew the Guru would pick up on it, too.

The Guru. Everyone always worshiped the Guru, with his commanding personality and his mind-reading skills, and his ability to hypnotize. Nobody paid the assistant any mind, even though he was also skillful; he'd been trained in magic, he knew sleight of hand and misdirection, and he could read body language very accurately.

The Guru was the one who'd given him a chance, despite him having had issues before that had landed him in jail for a couple of years. He had anger management issues that he knew. They'd been suppressed recently, but they had never gone away.

Anger and jealousy had flared inside him every time he watched a prospective customer's eyes flicker over him, unseeing, not even noticing him, as they waited breathlessly for the Guru and his powers. It was sickening. How could he live his entire life this way, never being respected, never being feared the way that he knew a few of the clients feared the Guru? That same fear was what he himself wanted and what he deserved.

It was so wrong that he hadn't yet achieved it.

At first, he'd tried to use the mental tricks and techniques that the Guru himself had taught him to try to subdue these emotions. But they hadn't worked. He'd realized cynically that the entire endeavor was simply an illusion. They were stupid techniques, just designed to make people fool themselves, and he was too clever for that.

He wasn't ready to fool himself, and his anger and jealousy were growing bigger and greedier by the day. In fact, it was as if he was turning into a completely different person, he thought. Now, his entire mind was focused on getting revenge – revenge on the world that had ignored him. He needed to prove that he was all-powerful, too, and to get the fear and respect he knew was due to him.

How to go about getting it?

The plan had come to him stealthily; a moment's idea had led to more. He knew he could pickpocket. It was one of the things he'd done before, in his past life. He knew he could steal. And it wasn't like his salary here was brilliant. Good, but not brilliant. And most of the day was just spent waiting around for those endless consultations to finish.

Gradually, over the months and then the years, the assistant had worked out the rhythm behind these consults and that they usually took either one hour or two hours, almost to the minute. That left him with a lot of spare time, and he'd started to use it. He'd gone out into the mall, and at first, he'd just stolen random items, taking them off people, feeling a glow of satisfaction at doing it without being seen. He'd loved the taste of this minor power.

Then, he'd realized he needed more, that this wasn't enough. It was power but not acknowledgment. He needed to see the reality that his intervention created in their lives.

When he'd seen the air tags in the shop, his answer had been there. In fact, it was at that moment he realized that he could do this, too. He could have power over people, just like the Guru. And, in fact, he wasn't going to stop at simple hypnosis. He wanted to try to drive people mad. To drive them to their death.

And so this exciting, rewarding rollercoaster ride had begun. And it had all seemed to go well, so perfectly well, right up until he'd seen that woman, with the edgy hairstyle and the bright jacket, outside the store this morning. And he'd seen the look in her eyes and read her body language, and he had known that something was up.

The more important question, of course, was why was she here. Did she suspect him?

He had been expecting people to come looking for him. That possibility had been top of mind. The police were generally stupid, and he had contempt for them, but the police were sometimes lucky. After all, they'd gotten lucky when they'd arrested him a few years ago.

And there were also private investigators, other avenues that could be explored. Maybe one of the women's parents had gone digging.

Maybe one of them had texted a friend about when this had started out, and they'd traced it back to the mall.

Or maybe it was just the police getting lucky at exactly the time he didn't need them to be.

This woman didn't look in the least like a policewoman. But she might be undercover. And earlier, he had seen two FBI officers walking through the mall. He'd assumed they were there for other reasons because they hadn't come near this side of the mall, but maybe he'd been wrong.

Now he came to think of it, one of those FBI officers had been a woman. Could it be her?

Perhaps it could. Yes, perhaps the puzzle pieces he had in his memory were now fitting together with what he saw in front of him.

He'd decided at the start of this exciting mission that if this happened, he needed to have a plan in place. And he'd thought for long hours about what the plan would be.

Would he deny it all? That might be dangerous because in his quest for adventure, for this experience of making others bend to his will, he had made some mistakes. He hadn't covered his tracks completely because this had developed so organically, and he'd astounded even himself with his success.

So he couldn't deny it.

That left one thing - run.

And he decided that before he ran, he was going to eliminate as many witnesses as he could. There were ways of getting a new ID and making a fresh start. They would all be much easier if nobody was left alive to say what he'd done or where he'd run.

The fingersmith hadn't been sure about the woman at first, but with his suspicions on the rise, he'd decided to take a little precaution as soon as she'd walked in.

Just something he could do to make sure.

He'd done that.

And then, of course, it had all exploded. Now, he was standing with a bloody knife in his hand and the Guru in a pool of his own blood on the floor. He was feeling a deep, visceral satisfaction in having used it. At last, he'd stabbed someone in the flesh; he'd delivered what he hoped was a killing blow. He'd finish the boss off in a moment because right now, it was time to eliminate the other witness.

The woman herself.

She was staring at him with fear in her eyes. Definitely not an experienced policewoman. And she had no gun. Probably, she'd just freeze on the spot while he stabbed her, like a deer in the headlights.

Only, as he lunged toward her with the knife, she surprised him. She turned and ran, powering her way out of the Guru's Grotto, the bell on the door jangling wildly as she wrenched it open.

He took a deep breath. This situation was out of control, and he needed to get it back, fast.

He had to chase her down.

How lucky it was that he'd taken out some insurance. At least he could be sure of finding her, he thought as he raced out of the shop, his shoes skidding on the tiles as he hurtled in pursuit.

CHAPTER TWENTY NINE

Cami couldn't believe how bad this had turned as she fled out of the Guru's Grotto, knowing that Radzi would be in hot pursuit with a bloodied knife in his hand. Now, it wasn't a case of solving the case. Now, it was all about saving her life because this killer had escalated. His violent urges had consumed him.

Connor could help, Connor could be here in a few minutes with police backup, but the problem was she hadn't had time to call him. For now, Cami knew she was on her own.

But she had one idea that she hoped would save her.

Getting among people. If other shoppers saw what was happening, they would do something. They'd intervene, they'd call the police, they'd be able to help.

But as she turned in the direction of the main mall, she saw this wasn't going to work.

The outer door, guarding the passage to the Guru's rooms, a door she hadn't even known was there because it had been open when she'd arrived, was now firmly closed. Reaching it, she pulled the handle down and shoved the door hard, but it was locked. Her heartbeat tripled.

He'd locked it earlier. He must have done it when he'd suspected who she was.

Now there was only one other way to turn, and that was left. And she had to be fast because he was right behind her, storming out of the waiting room as Cami ducked down the narrow passage that was her only bolthole now.

This looked like it was a new section of the mall under construction. She found herself running down a twisting passage that was lined with the empty shells of what would be small new stores. As she ran, the logical part of Cami's mind deduced that the smaller shops had been so successful that the mall was expanding on them and creating more, creating a little warren of stores, like a mini market. But they were empty and unoccupied, and as she ran further, she realized they were also largely unlit.

But at least the semi-darkness gave her an advantage, she thought. She could hunker down somewhere, hide away, and maybe he'd run straight past and give her more of a breathing space. If he did that, then she could run back to the Guru's rooms, she could barricade herself in that waiting room, or even in the main consulting room, and then she could make the calls she needed to.

At least she had a sketchy plan in place now.

So, needing to put it into action before Radzi closed in, Cami waited until she saw the next side passage ahead.

She checked behind her. Radzi wasn't in sight yet, although his footsteps were closing in.

She darted down the passage. Crouched behind a doorway in a tiny room and waited, holding her breath. Hopefully, he'd run straight past, and that would be it. She could let him get ahead, double back, and lock herself into the Guru's rooms.

But Radzi didn't run past.

He slowed, and then she heard the most terrifying sound in the world.

His footsteps, pacing slowly down the narrow passage toward her.

His voice, a singsong, taunting tone, calling out to her.

"Come here! Come here! I know exactly where you're hiding. I've gotten into your mind, into your brain. I'm going to be there forever, and you'll never be rid of me."

She felt a visceral terror grip her, a terror so sudden and powerful that it was temporarily paralyzing. For the first time, Cami truly understood how the victims must have felt when getting those messages. It was an overpowering sense of helplessness, of being targeted, of being seen. It was so traumatizing that she never, ever wanted to feel it again. Now it consumed her.

Now, she was in its thrall.

And then, finally, Cami's logical mind managed to break free from the fear. Thank goodness for that cold, logical voice in her mind that was almost always able to override the emotion and speak calmly and tell Cami exactly what to do.

And now, her logical mind was speaking over the flames of panic, acting like an icy extinguisher, giving Cami the facts over emotion.

"He put an air tag into your jacket. That's what he did. That's what you're getting now. The air tag messages, spoken instead of texted."

She inhaled a sharp, soundless gasp as she realized the truth. Of course, that was what he'd done. He'd had two opportunities when ushering her to the waiting chair and then again when he'd been shepherding her to the Guru's lair.

He'd realized that she wasn't a typical customer. Okay, so that hadn't been rocket science. And then, he'd done this as a precaution, together with locking the door to the main passage, so that he could chase her down in this semi-dark warren in a deadly game of hide and seek.

That was why, right now, he was turning into the side passage where she was cowering.

The knife made it so dangerous. The knife meant she couldn't risk him getting close.

Panic flaming, Cami burst out of her hiding place, running in a zigzag route into the ever-darker labyrinth of corridors.

He'd catch up with her; she knew that. Of course he would because he knew exactly where she was. But as she ran, she realized that although he was following, he wasn't pursuing her flat out. He was going just a little slower than he could have done. It was as if he was savoring this deadly dance, knowing that he had the ending of it in the bag.

As Cami skidded around another corner, her breath burning in her throat, her logical mind was fighting for prevalence again.

It was telling her that she needed to find this device. She needed to get hold of it. It was his weapon, and if she could find it, if she could get rid of it, then she had a chance.

Was it in her jacket?

Most likely. She didn't think it could be anywhere else. So then, all she had to do was rip off her jacket and flee away, and she'd lose him.

Cami was about to do that, and then, her logical mind spoke again.

This time, it came up with an idea so audacious and so daring that Cami was horrified.

"Find the device. And use it to trap him," her mind was telling her.

As her hands dug into her pockets, seeking the slim, round, slippery shape of the air tag, her brain was already grappling with the shocking thought she'd just had.

It would be dangerous. Impossibly so. She should just dispose of the air tag as fast as she could. This man had a knife, and if he got close enough, he'd use it.

But what if she escaped, and he ran for it? What if he had another plan in place to get away and flee the state, and he was now trying to make sure nobody could follow him too fast?

If he disappeared, then a dangerous man would be at large. He could start afresh somewhere else, he could steal more phones, he could harm more people. She knew what Connor would do in this situation. She knew what the brave choice was, and she had to try.

For the sake of all these women, she had to try to take him down.

Where was this air tag? It was difficult to search at a run. And behind her, those footsteps were gaining on her once more. She had the feeling that the mall's new area had a figure-eight layout and that she was running between its loops, but the problem was that in the semi-dark, and having run blindly, she was totally disoriented. She didn't know where she was or how to get back.

Plus, she was terrified that she'd take a wrong turn and run into a dead end. Then she'd be trapped, with a wall in front of her and a knife behind.

Cami knew she had to act fast. She couldn't keep running forever, and she couldn't risk being caught by the killer when he finally decided to stop his games. She needed a plan, and she needed it now.

She had to find this air tag. Without it, she wasn't going to win this. She was going to lose. But where was it? She'd checked both her side pockets, and it wasn't there.

The back pocket? Could he have somehow gotten it inside there? Surely not. But she had to try.

Cami reached behind her and dug her fingers into the back pocket, which was low down on the jacket and protected by a flap.

It wasn't there. Her heart plummeted. And then, remembering how deep that pocket was, she forced her hand further, twisting as she ran.

And, at last, her fingers closed around the air tag that she needed and that he'd hidden it in the most out-of-the-way place, in an incredibly skillful way. Somehow he'd opened that flap and slipped it inside, all in the time it had taken to usher her through a door.

Now she had a weapon, small but potentially lifesaving, gripped tightly in her hand, nestling in her palm.

And then, she saw an opportunity.

Ahead, she saw a white-painted row of small cubicles that must be going to be a restroom at some stage. And at the end of the row, there was a door with a key in the keyhole that must lead through to a store room or a janitor's room.

Could she do it? The scary part was that she'd have to hide along the way, and the cover was scanty. But she had to try because those footsteps were gaining.

Cami opened the far door and flung the air tag into the corner of the darkened room. Then, she closed it again as quietly as she could.

And then, she backtracked, cowering against the wall in one of the cubicles, knowing that the cover wasn't really good enough and that if he looked carefully to the side, he'd see her without a doubt.

She could only hope his focus on the chase led him forward.

Footsteps thudded on the concrete floor. A shadow loomed in the far doorway, visible in the faint overhead light.

He was coming fast. It was crunch time.

CHAPTER THIRTY

Cami flattened herself against the wall in the shadowy cubicle. Please, don't see me, she pleaded with her pursuer silently. Please, just rush past and go on in the door at the end.

As Radzi entered the row of cubicles, he was running.

But, as he neared her, the footsteps dropped back to a walk.

She heard his voice - singsong, taunting.

"Are you hiding from me?" The words were laced with malice. She could tell he was taking an intense pleasure in imagining her fear. "You don't have to hide, you know. You might as well come out because you're in my power now. My dark forces are surrounding you."

Cami held her breath, her heart beating rapidly in her chest. She stayed as still as possible, hoping he would just pass by and not notice her presence.

"Come out, come out, wherever you are," he taunted. And then, he continued with his breathless diatribe. "You'll see for yourself that I'm the real Guru. I'm not just an assistant. I'm not the one to be ignored and overlooked while people fawn over him and worship him. Oh, no. I'm a force to be taken seriously. More powerful than he ever was. Can you see that now? Do you understand how deadly I am?"

Step by step, he neared the place where she was hiding.

Cami held her breath, trying to make herself as small as possible. She wanted to close her eyes to make herself even more invisible but didn't dare to do it. Imagine if the next thing she felt was that knife slicing into her chest. No, her eyes were wide open and terrified, looking at the shadow of him through the gaps in the doorways. First, it lengthened, and then it shortened, and then it swung around as he passed under the weak overhead light.

Now, he was no more than a couple of yards from her.

Could he sense her heartbeat, the electric field of fear that seemed to be emanating from her? Cami did her best to keep stock still, even though she realized her legs were physically shaking. She forced them to stay strong. Even the tiniest tremor might be picked up on by this man, who had an acute sensitivity to his environment.

Radzi stopped right in front of the cubicle. If he looked sideways now, there was no way he wouldn't see her, and Cami's heart leaped into her throat. She could see his shadow through the gap in the doorway. There was no chance now, no chance at all for her. The game was up, and she hadn't yet had a chance to call Connor to get any help at all.

But then, she saw the pale light in his hand.

He was checking the phone screen. He was confirming the location of the air tag.

She waited, knowing that she now had the sliver of a chance because the light from the phone screen would decrease his ability to see into the shadows. It would help to blind him to his surroundings. And he was fully focused on his phone - ironically, just the same as his victims had been.

Now, if he could keep focused, and he moved forward just a few more steps into that room beyond, she had a chance.

He moved.

"Are you ready for me?" that singsong voice came again. "I'm so ready for you. This is going to be fun. The best fun I've ever had. It's time to make this real. You'll be the first, but you won't be the last."

And then, she heard the squeak as he pulled open the door and stepped inside.

Now, Cami thought. Now. She didn't have much time at all before he realized he was standing in an empty room. It was now a question of a few short seconds. That was all she would get.

Cami burst out of her hiding place and lunged toward the door, slamming it with all her strength, her fingers scrabbling for the key.

She needed to get it locked, but already, he'd realized that he'd walked into an empty room, and that she'd trapped him. With a howl of rage, he grabbed the handle from the inside, jerking it down, trying to push the door open, even as she got hold of the key.

The impact had rattled the key partway out of the keyhole. It wouldn't turn. It couldn't turn unless she got it all the way back in place, and she couldn't do that with him fighting her to get out again.

His voice rose to a shrill scream. The door shook. The handle was biting down into Cami's palm as she struggled to hold it up. She braced her Docs against the grainy concrete floor with all her might as she tried to prevent him from pushing that door open again.

Just let me turn the key, she begged to herself. Just let me turn it, and then all this will be over.

Gritting her teeth with the effort, she managed to get the key back into the keyhole again. But then, with a furious yell, he managed to jerk the door handle all the way down. She couldn't hold it. She had to let it go. She wasn't strong enough to hold it, and her palm was in agony, the bones bruised from the effort of trying.

Now, all she could do was to try to keep the door itself closed for long enough that she could turn the key.

Cami tried her best to channel Connor's calmness and focus. She tried to use all her strength and weight, such as it was, to hold that door.

And then, hoping it would go smoothly, hoping it wouldn't stick in the lock, she turned the key.

And it locked.

The click of that bolt sliding across was the most welcome sound she'd ever heard in her life. And it was only just in time because Radzi flung his weight against it so hard that the entire door shook, and she heard the lock mechanism squeak in protest. If she hadn't gotten it locked, he would have burst it open. Even with the lock in place, she might not have much time left.

"Let me out! Let me out! You can't do this! You're not allowed. This was never part of the plan!" he screamed, his voice now a shrill crescendo.

Cami backed away as she dialed Connor's number. He answered as soon as the call connected, his voice urgent.

"Cami. You okay?"

"I've got him," she said breathlessly. "I need backup, fast, as he might break out of where I've locked him. And he stabbed someone. His boss, in the Guru's Grotto. He needs help, fast." Were those all the salient facts? Had she told him everything she needed to in her panicked state? She hoped so.

"Send me your location. I'm going to get someone to you as fast as I can," Connor said. "Are you safe? I hear shouting and banging."

"For now," Cami said. "I've locked him in, and the door's holding."

"If it doesn't hold, run for help. And backup will be there as fast as possible. I'll call whoever's nearby. It should take a couple of minutes," he said. Then he hung up, clearly busy with getting things moving on his side.

Cami sent her location, her fingers shaking as she pressed the keys. Now he'd know where to rush to. And for the time being, the door was holding. It was withstanding his efforts to break through.

Radzi was screaming again.

"I'm in your mind. I'm controlling you. I'm in charge of your actions, and I'm telling you to open this door! Open it! Open it! Open it!"

Above his howling words, Cami could hear the shrill noise of sirens already on the way. Backup was speeding to the mall, and hopefully, police would be here in just a minute. She would be safe, and Radzi would be in their custody.

"Never again," she shouted back, keeping her gaze firmly fixed on that door. "Never again will you be able to make that work? You've done it for the last time. It's over now."

And, as she heard the crackle of radios and the sound of running feet approaching fast from the passageway, Cami knew that she'd done it.

He'd lost; they'd won. His reign of virtual terror, his hold over his victims' minds, had reached its end.

CHAPTER THIRTY ONE

Cami watched anxiously as the paramedics clustered around the Guru. They were working frantically on him, and she and Connor were the ones closest to the crime scene tape that was holding back the growing crowds. The scene was now being managed by three uniformed cops, with forensics on their way.

Cami was hoping that the man who'd given Radzi his second chance in life and who'd been the unfair target of his jealousy would survive.

At the moment, Radzi was in a police van, handcuffed and restrained, and on his way to a high-security prison cell. With overwhelming evidence against him so far, all the tracking of the air tags on his personal phone, two additional air tags on his person, and a further burner phone in his jacket, Cami knew the evidence would be overwhelming.

But as she watched the paramedics work on the Guru, she wondered if Radzi's mentor would survive. It had been a deep wound, and he'd lost a lot of blood.

The Guru might have had an unnerving insight into her own character, but it had been accurate. She couldn't fault his assessment of her motives or the way he'd immediately picked up when she'd said something untrue.

It was sad that he had been so focused on his own customers and so trusting of his assistant that he hadn't focused his instincts that way. If he had, he might have picked up on Radzi's swift descent into evil.

The paramedic looked around.

"Right," he said. "Let's get him on the stretcher. He has lost a lot of blood, but the knife missed anything vital. Lungs are okay, heart is okay, and he's stable."

Cami glanced at Connor, seeing that her boss looked as relieved as she felt.

"Glad to hear that," he said. "Good work, gentlemen."

"Thank you," Cami echoed. They moved away so that the paramedics could load the injured Guru and take him safely off to the hospital. Then, a team of forensic investigators were waiting to photograph and examine the scene where the crime had occurred, and the chase had started.

"Is there any news on Mindy Knowles?" she asked Connor, thinking of Radzi's third victim, and he nodded.

"Yes, I called the hospital half an hour ago. They said she's on the road to recovery. The concussion was milder than expected. They're monitoring her ribs, making sure they stay stable and don't do internal damage before they heal, and her broken leg required an operation with a pin, which has just been done, and she's recovering well." He paused. "I spoke to her parents after that and recommended that she get some psychological counseling to work through what happened. Something so intense might leave mental scars, as well as physical injuries."

Cami nodded soberly. This vengeful trail of destruction had caused shattered lives along its way. But at least, now, the pieces could be picked up, and the man himself had been arrested. For grieving families, that would provide closure, and she knew it would be important for his surviving victim, too. And for any others, he might have taunted without getting to the stage of making them break. She thought a lot of people would be glad to hear the news of this arrest.

There was still a lot of hard work to be done on the scene, but her job was over. And Connor was now looking at his phone, reading an incoming message.

"Jacenta is at the office. She's back from her vacation. And you need to speak to her now."

Cami nodded. She knew this couldn't be delayed any longer and that this discussion with her parole officer was extremely important.

She just didn't know, in light of recent events, how much she should tell her.

If Bill Oertel was involved in this, Cami didn't want to warn him. It would be too easy for him to destroy any evidence and cover his tracks.

And if he wasn't involved, and she named his name? Then it would put an innocent person at risk. She couldn't bear to be responsible for him being killed as Ethan and Liam had been.

The drive back to the FBI offices would take ten minutes.

She had a lot of thinking to do in that time.

*

Ten minutes later, to the minute, Cami was sitting in a private office on a floor of the FBI building that she'd never yet explored. This was where Jacinta worked from. The office had more personal touches to it than Connor's, she saw. There was a photo of a cute kid of about five years old, with dimples and a pink hair band in her hair. There was another photo of Jacenta holding the hand of a smiling man who Cami guessed was her husband. They were standing on top of a ski slope, ready to go down.

She had spoken to Jacinta several times over the past couple of months, but the conversations had been very focused on work and on Cami's own attitude and approach to her predicament. Not until now had she realized that Jacenta was a mom and also a lover of outdoor sports. She was a very multifaceted person, Cami realized and thought again how lucky she was to have her wisdom and insight. If only she knew what to do with it.

Wearing a blue work jacket, and a yellow top, the dark-haired, dark-eyed woman walked briskly in and sat down opposite, looking stylish but stern as she stared at Cami across the desk.

"Congratulations on this case," she said. "I've just read the notes and been briefed on the outcome. You acted very bravely, and you were extremely resourceful."

"Thank you," Cami said, feeling a glow of pride despite the tense circumstances. "I feel I'm growing into this role."

"Yes, you are. I'm observing exactly the same. I think this arrangement with the FBI has helped you to grow into your own personality and talents. I hope you might think of it as a future career because we need your skills here."

"I am thinking about it," Cami admitted, feeling on a happy cloud thanks to the praise.

"So, now," Jacenta said in a different tone, and Cami's stomach clenched as the happy cloud dissolved. Now it was time to get down to the real business of this meeting. "As we briefly discussed a few days ago, you've been doing some digging on your own. I'd like to hear about it. If possible, tell me everything."

Cami took a deep breath.

It was time to come clean. She needed to explain what had happened, and she was going to. Honestly, and knowing that Jacenta would keep the information privileged.

"I'll do that," she said. "But can we take a walk? I'd - I'd feel more comfortable outside these offices."

Jacinta nodded in understanding. "Let's take a walk down to the park on the corner," she said.

Heading out of the FBI offices, Cami had to admit it was not a good afternoon for a walk. The wind was blustering, snow was threatening, and it was freezing cold. But even so, she felt more comfortable talking about this matter outside those offices than inside.

As they walked, she explained to Jacenta exactly what had happened. The disappearance of her sister. The botching of the FBI case and how angry it had made her. The research she'd done and how she had found Liam's name, taken his laptop, gotten in touch. What he'd told her, and that he'd been murdered.

She saw how intense Jacenta looked when Cami told her that.

"I think Ethan was involved, too, in finding something about this out," Cami said, backtracking slightly to explain his role. And again, she told her all the information, full and frankly. It felt like a weight off her mind.

She no longer felt like she was carrying this burden alone. She knew that Jacinta would have her back, even though she had no idea how she'd take this problem on.

Even though there was one piece of the puzzle still missing so far. She wasn't willing to talk about Bill Oertel. Not yet.

"So, as you can see, I don't know what to do. I don't know who would be safe for me to tell about this and who's involved. I might know more soon," she added and saw Jacenta's gaze sharpen.

"What do you mean by that?" she asked.

Cami shook her head. "I can't say yet. There's one more thing I'm trying to find out in a subtle way. I don't want to put anyone at risk or warn anyone involved, so I'd like to finish the research on that first."

Jacenta looked thoughtful for a moment. "This is a difficult situation," she said. "I understand why you're being cautious. We need to tread carefully, but we also need to act because whatever is going on, they're clearly willing to go to extremes to protect it."

Cami nodded somberly.

"I'm going to think about this for a few days and then give you my opinion on what we should do," Jacenta said. "And in the meantime, if you hear anything more about this latest avenue you're researching, you need to tell me. Promise."

She stared at Cami sternly.

"I promise I will," she said.

She didn't know if her bait would be taken. It might not be possible to lure Bill Oertel in. He might never click on that email, and if he didn't, then Cami knew she'd need to use another way.

She didn't want to look for a different way, but she had to accept that there was going to be more trouble ahead. This was going to get worse and more dangerous before it got better - if it ever did.

EPILOGUE

"I'm home," Cami called, opening the apartment door. She felt pleased to be coming home to a place where a friendly person waited for her, who'd sent a smile emoji back when she'd said she was on her way. Kieran's reflective work jacket was hanging on the coat hook, and Kieran himself was in the kitchen.

"I just started making spaghetti bolognese," he called back. "And there's a bottle of red wine open. I'm using some for the food. Do you want a glass?"

"I'd love one. Let me see how you're doing dinner," Cami said, quickly taking off her FBI jacket and hanging it on the same coat stand. She took the gift she'd bought for Kieran out of her pocket and put it in the living room. Then she took her spare laptop out of her bag and plugged it in, and turned on her main laptop. And then, she hurried through to the kitchen.

"How was the case?" Kieran asked, handing her a glass of wine. He was frying onions - without crying, like she had done - and there was a container of ground beef standing by.

"We solved it," Cami said. "It got dangerous at the end, though. But luckily, the killer is in prison, and he'll never hurt anyone again."

"That's amazing," Kieran said. "Well done. I guess those situations must get very dangerous. After all, it's a life or death issue for the person who's committing those crimes."

"Exactly. A few decades in prison, for this guy," Cami said. The attempted murder of his boss, and the way he'd chased Cami with the knife, would add significantly to the sentence he was going to serve for the messages he'd sent his victims.

Kieran looked at the onions, stirred them, then added the ground beef to the pan. It smelled mouthwatering as it browned. It was wonderful to come home to a cooked meal on the go, with friendly company. But at the same time, she felt uneasy and rather self-conscious about her feelings for him.

"Listen," she said, remembering the guilty thoughts she'd had about taking up space in his living room.

"What?" he asked, adding a big splash of wine to the browning beef and then opening a tin of tomatoes.

"I don't want to impose on you here. I'm getting my exam results next week. I think when I get them, I need to move out. You've been so amazingly kind, but I - I can't stay here forever," she said, feeling her cheeks getting hot.

Kieran turned around from the stove and looked at her with a serious expression.

"Cami, I love having you here. I really enjoy your company. I want you to think of this as a long-term share. I don't want you to move out. Please, don't do that," he said.

"Well, I'm so grateful," she said. "But the problem is I'm taking up so much of your space. I feel bad using up your living room."

"There's another option there," he said hesitantly.

"What do you mean?" She felt stunned. There was only one thing he could mean, but was she totally wrong? This conversation was now heading in a direction that made a mix of warmth and nervousness start churning in her stomach.

"I mean, if you're not ready or you don't want to, it's absolutely fine. But if you wanted to maybe move into my bedroom - even just as friends - I'd be totally okay with that. In fact, I was getting ready to ask you if you wanted to do it."

Into his bedroom?

The implications of this were obvious, and now her face was boiling.

She wanted to take him up on this offer right now.

But then again, she didn't want to mess it up; she didn't know if it was too soon after Ethan's death, and she didn't know what the right or wrong thing to do would be in this situation.

"I really appreciate this offer," she said.

"I really mean it," he insisted.

"Perhaps we should work toward it? Over the next while?" she suggested. "I don't want to rush into anything. I don't want to damage what we have. But what you're suggesting sounds - well, it sounds exactly what I also want. A lot."

His face softened.

He turned away from the food, and his arms wrapped around her in a huge, warm hug, stroking her back, smoothing her hair. For a long while, this time, they stayed that way.

And then, from the living room, Cami heard a familiar ping.

"What's that?" Kieran asked as they finally let go of each other.

It was her laptop, now powered up and sending notifications out.

That ping? It was an alarm she'd set to go off, and she knew what it meant. Excitement flared inside her as she rushed through to check.

"Kieran!" she called. "Look here! My email bait worked! Bill Oertel clicked on the link. He went through to the site!"

Now, at last, she had a backdoor into his machine. She could take a step further into the darkness that lay beyond these murders.

Now, she could see who Bill Oertel really was and what he'd been doing.

NOW AVAILABLE!

JUST LEAVE
(A Cami Lark FBI Suspense Thriller—Book 9)

With her tattoos and piercings, MIT tech genius Cami Lark is rebellious and anti-authoritarian—and finds herself in deep trouble when she hacks the FBI. Faced with the choice of prison or aiding the BAU to hunt down serial killers, Cami reluctantly partners. But when a string of women turn up killed with seemingly no connection, Cami senses some new technology is behind it, and linking these women. She knows she must outsmart the killer before he claims his next one....

"A masterpiece of thriller and mystery."
—Books and Movie Reviews, Roberto Mattos (re Once Gone)

JUST LEAVE (A Cami Lark FBI Suspense Thriller—Book 9) is the ninth novel in a new series by #1 bestseller and USA Today bestselling author Blake Pierce, whose bestseller Once Gone (a free download) has received over 7,000 five star ratings and reviews.

A page-turning and harrowing crime thriller featuring a brilliant and tortured FBI agent, the CAMI LARK series is a riveting mystery, packed with non-stop action, suspense, twists and turns, revelations, and driven by a breakneck pace that will keep you flipping pages late into the night. Fans of Rachel Caine, Teresa Driscoll and Robert Dugoni are sure to fall in love.

Future books will be available soon.

"An edge of your seat thriller in a new series that keeps you turning pages! ...So many twists, turns and red herrings... I can't wait to see what happens next."
—Reader review (Her Last Wish)

"A strong, complex story about two FBI agents trying to stop a serial killer. If you want an author to capture your attention and have you guessing, yet trying to put the pieces together, Pierce is your author!"

—Reader review (Her Last Wish)

"A typical Blake Pierce twisting, turning, roller coaster ride suspense thriller. Will have you turning the pages to the last sentence of the last chapter!!!"
—Reader review (City of Prey)

"Right from the start we have an unusual protagonist that I haven't seen done in this genre before. The action is nonstop... A very atmospheric novel that will keep you turning pages well into the wee hours."
—Reader review (City of Prey)

"Everything that I look for in a book... a great plot, interesting characters, and grabs your interest right away. The book moves along at a breakneck pace and stays that way until the end. Now on go I to book two!"
—Reader review (Girl, Alone)

"Exciting, heart pounding, edge of your seat book... a must read for mystery and suspense readers!"
—Reader review (Girl, Alone)

Blake Pierce

Blake Pierce is the USA Today bestselling author of the RILEY PAGE mystery series, which includes seventeen books. Blake Pierce is also the author of the MACKENZIE WHITE mystery series, comprising fourteen books; of the AVERY BLACK mystery series, comprising six books; of the KERI LOCKE mystery series, comprising five books; of the MAKING OF RILEY PAIGE mystery series, comprising six books; of the KATE WISE mystery series, comprising seven books; of the CHLOE FINE psychological suspense mystery, comprising six books; of the JESSIE HUNT psychological suspense thriller series, comprising thirty-one books; of the AU PAIR psychological suspense thriller series, comprising three books; of the ZOE PRIME mystery series, comprising six books; of the ADELE SHARP mystery series, comprising sixteen books, of the EUROPEAN VOYAGE cozy mystery series, comprising six books; of the LAURA FROST FBI suspense thriller, comprising eleven books; of the ELLA DARK FBI suspense thriller, comprising twenty-one books (and counting); of the A YEAR IN EUROPE cozy mystery series, comprising nine books, of the AVA GOLD mystery series, comprising six books; of the RACHEL GIFT mystery series, comprising thirteen books (and counting); of the VALERIE LAW mystery series, comprising nine books (and counting); of the PAIGE KING mystery series, comprising eight books (and counting); of the MAY MOORE mystery series, comprising eleven books; of the CORA SHIELDS mystery series, comprising eight books (and counting); of the NICKY LYONS mystery series, comprising eight books (and counting), of the CAMI LARK mystery series, comprising nine books (and counting), of the AMBER YOUNG mystery series, comprising seven books (and counting), of the DAISY FORTUNE mystery series, comprising five books (and counting), of the FIONA RED mystery series, comprising nine books (and counting), of the FAITH BOLD mystery series, comprising eight books (and counting), of the JULIETTE HART mystery series, comprising five books (and counting), of the MORGAN CROSS mystery series, comprising seven books (and counting), and of the new FINN WRIGHT mystery series, comprising five books (and counting).

An avid reader and lifelong fan of the mystery and thriller genres,

Blake loves to hear from you, so please feel free to visit www.blakepierceauthor.com to learn more and stay in touch.

BOOKS BY BLAKE PIERCE

FINN WRIGHT MYSTERY SERIES
WHEN YOU'RE MINE (Book #1)
WHEN YOU'RE SAFE (Book #2)
WHEN YOU'RE CLOSE (Book #3)
WHEN YOU'RE SLEEPING (Book #4)
WHEN YOU'RE SANE (Book #5)

MORGAN CROSS MYSTERY SERIES
FOR YOU (Book #1)
FOR RAGE (Book #2)
FOR LUST (Book #3)
FOR WRATH (Book #4)
FOREVER (Book #5)
FOR US (Book #6)
FOR NOW (Book #7)

JULIETTE HART MYSTERY SERIES
NOTHING TO FEAR (Book #1)
NOTHING THERE (Book #2)
NOTHING WATCHING (Book #3)
NOTHING HIDING (Book #4)
NOTHING LEFT (Book #5)

FAITH BOLD MYSTERY SERIES
SO LONG (Book #1)
SO COLD (Book #2)
SO SCARED (Book #3)
SO NORMAL (Book #4)
SO FAR GONE (Book #5)
SO LOST (Book #6)
SO ALONE (Book #7)
SO FORGOTTEN (Book #8)

FIONA RED MYSTERY SERIES

LET HER GO (Book #1)
LET HER BE (Book #2)
LET HER HOPE (Book #3)
LET HER WISH (Book #4)
LET HER LIVE (Book #5)
LET HER RUN (Book #6)
LET HER HIDE (Book #7)
LET HER BELIEVE (Book #8)
LET HER FORGET (Book #9)

DAISY FORTUNE MYSTERY SERIES
NEED YOU (Book #1)
CLAIM YOU (Book #2)
CRAVE YOU (Book #3)
CHOOSE YOU (Book #4)
CHASE YOU (Book #5)

AMBER YOUNG MYSTERY SERIES
ABSENT PITY (Book #1)
ABSENT REMORSE (Book #2)
ABSENT FEELING (Book #3)
ABSENT MERCY (Book #4)
ABSENT REASON (Book #5)
ABSENT SANITY (Book #6)
ABSENT LIFE (Book #7)

CAMI LARK MYSTERY SERIES
JUST ME (Book #1)
JUST OUTSIDE (Book #2)
JUST RIGHT (Book #3)
JUST FORGET (Book #4)
JUST ONCE (Book #5)
JUST HIDE (Book #6)
JUST NOW (Book #7)
JUST HOPE (Book #8)
JUST LEAVE (Book #9)

NICKY LYONS MYSTERY SERIES
ALL MINE (Book #1)
ALL HIS (Book #2)

ALL HE SEES (Book #3)
ALL ALONE (Book #4)
ALL FOR ONE (Book #5)
ALL HE TAKES (Book #6)
ALL FOR ME (Book #7)
ALL IN (Book #8)

CORA SHIELDS MYSTERY SERIES
UNDONE (Book #1)
UNWANTED (Book #2)
UNHINGED (Book #3)
UNSAID (Book #4)
UNGLUED (Book #5)
UNSTABLE (Book #6)
UNKNOWN (Book #7)
UNAWARE (Book #8)

MAY MOORE SUSPENSE THRILLER
NEVER RUN (Book #1)
NEVER TELL (Book #2)
NEVER LIVE (Book #3)
NEVER HIDE (Book #4)
NEVER FORGIVE (Book #5)
NEVER AGAIN (Book #6)
NEVER LOOK BACK (Book #7)
NEVER FORGET (Book #8)
NEVER LET GO (Book #9)
NEVER PRETEND (Book #10)
NEVER HESITATE (Book #11)

PAIGE KING MYSTERY SERIES
THE GIRL HE PINED (Book #1)
THE GIRL HE CHOSE (Book #2)
THE GIRL HE TOOK (Book #3)
THE GIRL HE WISHED (Book #4)
THE GIRL HE CROWNED (Book #5)
THE GIRL HE WATCHED (Book #6)
THE GIRL HE WANTED (Book #7)
THE GIRL HE CLAIMED (Book #8)

VALERIE LAW MYSTERY SERIES
NO MERCY (Book #1)
NO PITY (Book #2)
NO FEAR (Book #3)
NO SLEEP (Book #4)
NO QUARTER (Book #5)
NO CHANCE (Book #6)
NO REFUGE (Book #7)
NO GRACE (Book #8)
NO ESCAPE (Book #9)

RACHEL GIFT MYSTERY SERIES
HER LAST WISH (Book #1)
HER LAST CHANCE (Book #2)
HER LAST HOPE (Book #3)
HER LAST FEAR (Book #4)
HER LAST CHOICE (Book #5)
HER LAST BREATH (Book #6)
HER LAST MISTAKE (Book #7)
HER LAST DESIRE (Book #8)
HER LAST REGRET (Book #9)
HER LAST HOUR (Book #10)
HER LAST SHOT (Book #11)
HER LAST PRAYER (Book #12)
HER LAST LIE (Book #13)

AVA GOLD MYSTERY SERIES
CITY OF PREY (Book #1)
CITY OF FEAR (Book #2)
CITY OF BONES (Book #3)
CITY OF GHOSTS (Book #4)
CITY OF DEATH (Book #5)
CITY OF VICE (Book #6)

A YEAR IN EUROPE
A MURDER IN PARIS (Book #1)
DEATH IN FLORENCE (Book #2)
VENGEANCE IN VIENNA (Book #3)
A FATALITY IN SPAIN (Book #4)

ELLA DARK FBI SUSPENSE THRILLER
GIRL, ALONE (Book #1)
GIRL, TAKEN (Book #2)
GIRL, HUNTED (Book #3)
GIRL, SILENCED (Book #4)
GIRL, VANISHED (Book 5)
GIRL ERASED (Book #6)
GIRL, FORSAKEN (Book #7)
GIRL, TRAPPED (Book #8)
GIRL, EXPENDABLE (Book #9)
GIRL, ESCAPED (Book #10)
GIRL, HIS (Book #11)
GIRL, LURED (Book #12)
GIRL, MISSING (Book #13)
GIRL, UNKNOWN (Book #14)
GIRL, DECEIVED (Book #15)
GIRL, FORLORN (Book #16)
GIRL, REMADE (Book #17)
GIRL, BETRAYED (Book #18)
GIRL, BOUND (Book #19)
GIRL, REFORMED (Book #20)
GIRL, REBORN (Book #21)

LAURA FROST FBI SUSPENSE THRILLER
ALREADY GONE (Book #1)
ALREADY SEEN (Book #2)
ALREADY TRAPPED (Book #3)
ALREADY MISSING (Book #4)
ALREADY DEAD (Book #5)
ALREADY TAKEN (Book #6)
ALREADY CHOSEN (Book #7)
ALREADY LOST (Book #8)
ALREADY HIS (Book #9)
ALREADY LURED (Book #10)
ALREADY COLD (Book #11)

EUROPEAN VOYAGE COZY MYSTERY SERIES
MURDER (AND BAKLAVA) (Book #1)
DEATH (AND APPLE STRUDEL) (Book #2)
CRIME (AND LAGER) (Book #3)

MISFORTUNE (AND GOUDA) (Book #4)
CALAMITY (AND A DANISH) (Book #5)
MAYHEM (AND HERRING) (Book #6)

ADELE SHARP MYSTERY SERIES
LEFT TO DIE (Book #1)
LEFT TO RUN (Book #2)
LEFT TO HIDE (Book #3)
LEFT TO KILL (Book #4)
LEFT TO MURDER (Book #5)
LEFT TO ENVY (Book #6)
LEFT TO LAPSE (Book #7)
LEFT TO VANISH (Book #8)
LEFT TO HUNT (Book #9)
LEFT TO FEAR (Book #10)
LEFT TO PREY (Book #11)
LEFT TO LURE (Book #12)
LEFT TO CRAVE (Book #13)
LEFT TO LOATHE (Book #14)
LEFT TO HARM (Book #15)
LEFT TO RUIN (Book #16)

THE AU PAIR SERIES
ALMOST GONE (Book#1)
ALMOST LOST (Book #2)
ALMOST DEAD (Book #3)

ZOE PRIME MYSTERY SERIES
FACE OF DEATH (Book#1)
FACE OF MURDER (Book #2)
FACE OF FEAR (Book #3)
FACE OF MADNESS (Book #4)
FACE OF FURY (Book #5)
FACE OF DARKNESS (Book #6)

A JESSIE HUNT PSYCHOLOGICAL SUSPENSE SERIES
THE PERFECT WIFE (Book #1)
THE PERFECT BLOCK (Book #2)
THE PERFECT HOUSE (Book #3)
THE PERFECT SMILE (Book #4)

THE PERFECT LIE (Book #5)
THE PERFECT LOOK (Book #6)
THE PERFECT AFFAIR (Book #7)
THE PERFECT ALIBI (Book #8)
THE PERFECT NEIGHBOR (Book #9)
THE PERFECT DISGUISE (Book #10)
THE PERFECT SECRET (Book #11)
THE PERFECT FAÇADE (Book #12)
THE PERFECT IMPRESSION (Book #13)
THE PERFECT DECEIT (Book #14)
THE PERFECT MISTRESS (Book #15)
THE PERFECT IMAGE (Book #16)
THE PERFECT VEIL (Book #17)
THE PERFECT INDISCRETION (Book #18)
THE PERFECT RUMOR (Book #19)
THE PERFECT COUPLE (Book #20)
THE PERFECT MURDER (Book #21)
THE PERFECT HUSBAND (Book #22)
THE PERFECT SCANDAL (Book #23)
THE PERFECT MASK (Book #24)
THE PERFECT RUSE (Book #25)
THE PERFECT VENEER (Book #26)
THE PERFECT PEOPLE (Book #27)
THE PERFECT WITNESS (Book #28)
THE PERFECT APPEARANCE (Book #29)
THE PERFECT TRAP (Book #30)
THE PERFECT EXPRESSION (Book #31)

CHLOE FINE PSYCHOLOGICAL SUSPENSE SERIES
NEXT DOOR (Book #1)
A NEIGHBOR'S LIE (Book #2)
CUL DE SAC (Book #3)
SILENT NEIGHBOR (Book #4)
HOMECOMING (Book #5)
TINTED WINDOWS (Book #6)

KATE WISE MYSTERY SERIES
IF SHE KNEW (Book #1)
IF SHE SAW (Book #2)
IF SHE RAN (Book #3)

IF SHE HID (Book #4)
IF SHE FLED (Book #5)
IF SHE FEARED (Book #6)
IF SHE HEARD (Book #7)

THE MAKING OF RILEY PAIGE SERIES
WATCHING (Book #1)
WAITING (Book #2)
LURING (Book #3)
TAKING (Book #4)
STALKING (Book #5)
KILLING (Book #6)

RILEY PAIGE MYSTERY SERIES
ONCE GONE (Book #1)
ONCE TAKEN (Book #2)
ONCE CRAVED (Book #3)
ONCE LURED (Book #4)
ONCE HUNTED (Book #5)
ONCE PINED (Book #6)
ONCE FORSAKEN (Book #7)
ONCE COLD (Book #8)
ONCE STALKED (Book #9)
ONCE LOST (Book #10)
ONCE BURIED (Book #11)
ONCE BOUND (Book #12)
ONCE TRAPPED (Book #13)
ONCE DORMANT (Book #14)
ONCE SHUNNED (Book #15)
ONCE MISSED (Book #16)
ONCE CHOSEN (Book #17)

MACKENZIE WHITE MYSTERY SERIES
BEFORE HE KILLS (Book #1)
BEFORE HE SEES (Book #2)
BEFORE HE COVETS (Book #3)
BEFORE HE TAKES (Book #4)
BEFORE HE NEEDS (Book #5)
BEFORE HE FEELS (Book #6)
BEFORE HE SINS (Book #7)

BEFORE HE HUNTS (Book #8)
BEFORE HE PREYS (Book #9)
BEFORE HE LONGS (Book #10)
BEFORE HE LAPSES (Book #11)
BEFORE HE ENVIES (Book #12)
BEFORE HE STALKS (Book #13)
BEFORE HE HARMS (Book #14)

AVERY BLACK MYSTERY SERIES
CAUSE TO KILL (Book #1)
CAUSE TO RUN (Book #2)
CAUSE TO HIDE (Book #3)
CAUSE TO FEAR (Book #4)
CAUSE TO SAVE (Book #5)
CAUSE TO DREAD (Book #6)

KERI LOCKE MYSTERY SERIES
A TRACE OF DEATH (Book #1)
A TRACE OF MURDER (Book #2)
A TRACE OF VICE (Book #3)
A TRACE OF CRIME (Book #4)
A TRACE OF HOPE (Book #5)

Made in the USA
Monee, IL
29 August 2023

41807816R00100